As the Worm Turns

AS THE WORM TURNS

BRIAN ROSENBERGER

Blue Room Publishing
Conshohocken, Pennsylvania, USA

As the Worm Turns and all contents within are works of fiction. Names, characters, places and incidents either are the product of the author's imagination or are used fictitiously. Any resemblance to actual persons, living or dead, events or locales is entirely coincidental.

Published in the United States by
Blue Room Publishing.

www.blueroompublishing.com

Photography & cover design by Laura Ostman
Edited by Michael Ferrari

ISBN 978-0-9843006-3-1
LCCN 2009913285

Printed in the United States of America.

DEDICATION

For all the ghouls and friends of ghouls,
the fiends and fans of tooth and claw,
the midnight creepers, the cemetery reapers
the revenge minded
with a fever in their head,
an inferno in their eyes,
a knife in their hand and heart,
For those in the back of the class,
the back of the bus,
the back of the hearse,
For the scary, the scarred and the scared.
the underground, the underclass,
and the overworked,
but mostly it's for me
but I thank you
all the same.

"One good act of vengeance deserves another."

--John Jefferson

CONTENTS

NOTES FROM THE LAB
AN INTRODUCTION

Being a mad scientist with an extremely popular spookshow isn't easy.

Aside from all the problems that come along with deranged experiments, unfit laboratory assistants and noxious fumes from radioactive chemicals, there are the unruly monster movie crowds, the ghoulishly glamorous dancing girls as well as the creation and execution of new and exciting magic tricks. It can take up a monstrous amount of time. All of my time! And one thing that seems to really *suffer* for it (and not just my personal relationships) is my reading time!

Being an avid reader with a blisteringly busy schedule can be tough. How can I find the time to read a thousand-page book when I can't even get these zombies delivered to Haiti on deadline?

Well, Praise Satan for Brian Rosenberger! New blood has arrived on the literary horror scene with a refreshing approach to churning stomachs and boiling brains—he gets it done in a matter of pages! Hell, some of the stories in this creepy compendium are only pages-long and they leave an impact that is hard to shake. His story "The Guests" is only one solitary page and it's one of the most harrowing Halloween tales that I've ever read! These stories are perfect for those with Attention

Deficit Disorder. The MTV (Monster Television, of course) generation should gobble them up with relish.

I'm not going to ruin any surprises or snuff any shocks by giving you a detailed rundown of the stories within these pages. You are about to embark on that journey and find out for yourself...hopefully while all alone with very few lights on in the house.

But I will say that I really enjoyed taking a terrifying trip with the imagination of Brian Rosenberger, through all of the twisted turns to the dark places (and sometimes laughing out loud on the way there).

Even the familiar seems unfamiliar under his pen. As you will find the schoolyard and the small town transformed into the phantasmagoric. Lovecraftian horrors leave splatterpunk traces along the walls of these once normal, now *different* dark places.

I had never heard of this writer before he asked me to write the foreword to this book, but I'm sure we will all be hearing much about him in the near future. I felt a thrill reading this book that was much like when I discovered the *Books of Blood* by Clive Barker in the early '80s.

Thanks to Brian, a fresh wound has opened up in the literary world and is spilling copious amounts of ghoulish gore in sickly, scintillating stories on virgin, yet putrid parchments. So settle in, turn the lights down low and get ready for a real treat: A new*fang*led talent ready to *Scare the Yell Outta You!*

Enjoy, you sick and depraved little Boils and Ghouls!

--Prof. Morte

Professor Morte has been performing for most of his afterlife in various parts of the world. Currently, the Professor is the ghost host with the most of the Silver Scream Spookshow, haunting At-

lanta's Plaza Theatre the last weekend of every month. With a cast of creepy, colorful characters, the Spookshow mixes scares, comedy, dance numbers and horrifically hip hijinks. A classic horror film follows each show giving guests more boo for the buck!

Visit www.silverscreamspookshow.com where the screams are always free.

AS THE WORM TURNS

It walked. Nothing could slow its progress, shark-like in its determination. The crowd kept a safe distance, silently watching in anticipation like mice, dreading the trap. Its head moved side to side, seeing only potential victims. Today's prey had already been targeted. The others would have to wait. Its mission was one of destruction. Muscles tensed. One muscular arm reached out and in a motion usually reserved for Nature documentaries, flesh met steel. The other kids laughed as the victim bounced off the locker to the floor. Books and papers scattered like confetti in a celebration of survival; it could have been much worse. It grunted, paused, waiting for an invitation, an excuse for further violence, and moved on, eyes ever alert for the next accident it could make happen.

It was called Cow Killer, though rarely to its face. Cow Killer's real name was Donald Oscar Monroe. To the majority of the Lew Wallace High School student population, he was simply Monroe. He was also known as Asshole, Cocksucker, Big Dumb Bastard and Prick. Hardly terms of affection and usually said under concealed breath and well out of Monroe's listening distance. Rule Number 6 in the high school survivor guide: Never insult the toughest kid in school to his face unless you desired spending the rest of your life dining through a straw.

Topping six feet and close to two hundred pounds, Monroe was a mean son of a bitch. The Monroe family could not only stack shit tractor-wheel high but they also dared to dress it up in jeans and t-shirts. Monroe was walking excrement, a turd with a mean streak. Rubbing shoulders with him was like having diarrhea and realizing you're out of TP. It was a lose-lose situation. Rabid possums had more personality. Mad dogs were put out of their misery; Monroe lived to inflict it.

Monroe picked up the Cow Killer nickname during our junior year. We were in the same grade, meaning I had survived his particular blend of hostility and stupidity for years. By high school, bully practice was over; Monroe had turned pro. For the most part, I kept under his radar, getting only the occasion slap to the head or kick ball to the face—the equivalent of a playground drive-by—and the usual assortment of insults. But terms like Douche bag or Pussyboy lost their effectiveness after the third or fourth time. Monroe wasn't clever enough to come up with new material on his own. I had my own keep-from-getting-your-ass-kicked detector, and I made sure its batteries never died.

Rumor in the hallways had it that Monroe accidentally shot a cow during deer season. Could happen to anyone right? But to this day, it's the only report of bovine assassination I'm aware of aside from UFO attacks. Maybe it was a case of self-defense or maybe the cow took one look at Monroe's Neanderthal brow and stump of a nose and saw a potential suitor. There were other rumors that it wasn't an accident, that he transformed the cow into hamburger as a result of multiple gunshots to the head. But those were just rumors.

There was also a rumor that Steve Kelley called Monroe Cow Killer to his face. Did it happen? Kelley did get the shit kicked out of him during gym class. Actually, it was right after, in the shower room. Witnesses said they saw more offense out of the debate team. Kelley never stood a chance. I saw the aftermath. It wasn't pretty. Kelly's eye looked like week-old roast beef, and that was the good one. The other made the cafeteria casserole look appetizing. The other rumor was that someone paid Monroe to beat up Kelley. A high school hit. But rumors like that were as common as cigarette butts in the girls' restroom.

All fairly common high school shit, at least the fighting and gossip. Cow killing on the other hand? My high school years probably weren't that much different from Joe or Jane Adolescence. Just going through the motions, waiting for that final bell to ring, just trying to survive. A real yawner. Then I met Orm.

Orm Totes, as I would later learn, was named after some Spanish sea captain in the 1400's I'd never heard of. I thought Ormanual was one of those soft-core porn movies on HBO or Showtime I sometimes was lucky enough to watch. Back then Orm didn't know what I was talking about (but he would learn). Orm had big goldfish eyes, and I mean the type of goldfish that belong in a tank marked "genetic experiment" in an Area 51 aquarium. Orm had some big peepers made even worse by his glasses, which looked like a leftover Halloween prop.

Orm was a new kid. Tall, gangly. He could have made a good power forward if he gained a few more pounds. His crouching posture didn't suggest he was much of a jock though. I had seen him around, but he didn't hang with any of the three or four people I loosely called my friends; I don't think he hung out with anyone. He was always wearing a green Army jacket and green Converse. I always thought that was odd cause everyone else wore black Cons. It was the *in* thing. I stuck to my Reeboks. The only *in* thing I was concerned about was getting in some cheerleader's panties. A sexist remark. She didn't have to be a cheerleader.

My first contact with Orm was over a dead body. Our small town didn't have a bookstore, just a corner drug store that carried national magazines and newspapers. For some reason, people stuck their gum under the counter; it looked like Juicy Fruit-flavored tumors were growing. The store had one security camera that everyone knew was just a hunk of plastic mounted on a wall. Hiring Ernie Rednose, one of the town drunks to stand guard, would've been more effective, if they could have caught Ernie between sips. Ernie spent so much time sitting in front of the store he was considered a local landmark. I went to the drug store mainly to buy comics and to skim through the skin mags when no one was looking. The store got new shipments in on Thursdays. I had wandered over to the racks and was greeted by a skinless skull smiling in my direction, the cover of that month's *Fangoria*. Behind the magazine stood Orm.

We started talking and discovered a mutual interest in things that go splat. We talked about Argento, Romero and Cronenberg and how Hollywood horror sucked. Orm expressed how the best stuff came out of Asia, name-dropping films I'd only read about. We both loved *Re-Animator*. My eyes grew as large as his peeps when he confessed to having copies of everything he mentioned. He couldn't hide his enthusiasm, one I also shared. We made plans to get together that weekend and became fast friends over the next few weeks watching people die in the most violent ways imaginable. It was great.

His family was great, too. There was a family resemblance; they all had the same complexion, kind of like a can of mushroom soup but without the mushrooms. His mother Velda had the same pigment (only with smaller eyes) but on her it looked good. Damn good. She was hot, super-model thin with breasts that dared you not to stare. The word exotic was made for her. She had long black hair that seemed to move like ocean waves. She spoke with a thick accent, maybe Boston, definitely not from the Midwest. Orm shared it, too.

Velda was a definite New Ager, listening to music that sounded like whales mating. The house was decorated in early Zodiac. All kinds of weird astrological stuff on the walls, charts and symbols and primitive masks. She was big on home health care, homeopathic medicine, weeds and flowers no one would think to eat. She had written a few books on the subject, mostly self-published but with a foreign distributor. Her books had been translated in five languages.

His dad, Jeb, was big, like a bear with male pattern baldness, and worked in sales. He was always on the road. He was a worm farmer, swear to God. Raised them in beds in the Totes' basement. Orm helped out, made sure the worms were fed and the soil rotated. Orm had a way with those worms. You'd think he could teach them tricks the way they responded to him. He said he could call them. I think they just responded to the smell of food, a mix of potato peelings, carrots, cabbage, banana peels, grapefruit and coffee grounds. Orm said it added protein to their diet to make them grow. They were big, bigger than anything I'd ever used for bait. He said it was an old family recipe. That and their breeding accounted for their size. Orm said this particular worm had been bred from the Bungum Worm, also know as the Giant Beach Worm. He said the Bungum grew to be 8 feet long. I said he was full of shit and he only wished he had even an 8-inch worm. In his pants. We both laughed at that.

Worm breeder or not, Jeb was very educated with multiple degrees, but was too much of a people person to spend life working in a lab. He sold his worms and Vend-A-Bait machines throughout the Midwest. Made a good living at it, too. Orm, along with his worm wrangling abilities, inherited his father's eyes. Jeb's glasses looked like a pair of beer mugs. He blinked a thousand times a second. Life must have been like a strobe light for him. Nice enough guy. He'd give us 20 bucks on the weekends when he was around and say with a smile, "Stay away from trouble and girls looking for a husband."

No one really saw much of the parents in town. Some people are social butterflies; I think the Totes family enjoyed being moths. They lived at the old Markland farm, just a little ways out of town. A long bike ride but not impossible. Old man Markland was another of the town's drunk. Rumor was his grandfather had lost the property in a pool hall bet. Granddad disappeared shortly there after and the bank foreclosed. Old man Markland was better known as Mushmouth as he had only two teeth and they lived on opposite sides of his tongue. As a farmer, he made a much better alcoholic. The barn was still standing, functioning as a garage. I never saw any farm equipment. No tractor or plow just a few stray chickens. Orm said they were wild. The only thing I knew about farms was … Hell, I didn't know a damn thing about farms except calling someone a pig farmer was always pretty funny whether they raised swine or not.

Orm always liked staying over at my house. Said it was like a real family, which is odd considering my dad wasn't around. He died years ago, a drunk driving accident. Witnesses said he staggered out of Ye Olde Shack, a local tavern, hopped in his Mustang and headed for home. He never made it. At some point, between the bar and home, he stopped to take a piss. He relieved himself in the woods but staggered too far into the road and was struck by an ambulance rushing to the Watson place. Mrs. Watson, who wore her hair like Elsa Lanchester in the *Bride of Frankenstein,* suffered a heart attack or stroke on a monthly basis. It was never serious; she just liked the attention. Anyway the ambulance caught Dad mid zip and knocked him 30 feet into the cemetery where he landed headfirst on a tombstone. The medical examiner said he died of a broken neck. He was buried within spitting distance of that very spot. Mrs. Watson had even recovered enough to attend the funeral.

Mom didn't mind Ormanual (she always called him Ormanual) staying over. We'd order pizza. Orm loved pizza, but always insisted on anchovies. As a result, we'd get half-and-half. He got anchovies, and I settled for pepperoni. Sometimes my mom would join us and we would play cards for hours. And then kick back and watch whatever straight-to-video horror film was that week's new release. After three weekends of watching the likes of *Street Trash, Redneck Zombies* and *Dolls,* Mom learned to skip movie time. It then became time to educate Orm to the wonders of late-night cable. *National Geographic* had nothing on us.

We settled into a pretty good pattern, hanging out as often as possible. School was school. The semester ended. We had a few days off. Time to catch up on the new releases and watch and re-watch the classics--

Demons, Crawlspace, From Beyond, The Fog. It was a marathon of the macabre with no finish line in sight. When school resumed, Orm and I finally ended up in a class together: biology. I got lucky. My lab partner was Annette "The Hottie" Schottelkotte. Not only was she a cheerleader, but she smelled better than all the bubble gum in the world. She was Grade-A jerk-off material. Hair as red as fake blood and a smile hiding lips sensual enough to make a dead man rise. She made me feel prehistoric, petrified wood hiding in my pants. Orm joked her Indian name would be Spread Eagle. I was hoping that was true. Orm, on the other hand, had nothing to laugh about; his partner was Monroe.

The trouble started after the first quiz. Orm failed it miserably. The problem being Monroe cheated off Orm's paper. Monroe didn't take it well. He caught Orm in the stairwell going to the library and explained in as much detail as his limited imagination would allow what would happen if the next quiz ended with the same result. Orm took everything in stride. I was more upset than he was. I'd seen the aftermath of Hurricane Monroe. Kelley's face still bore a scar. I remember Orm saying, "Dude, the scariest thing about Monroe, aside from his breath, is his body odor. What's he got against soap? Besides, I'll breeze the next quiz. No fear."

True to his word, Orm aced the next quiz. We had to label a worm's anatomy. Can you say no brainer? I even got a B+. Monroe had been suspended for skipping classes. That's punishment--you get to miss even more classes.

Monroe returned to school, his short vacation working wonders for his personality. He developed a habit of kicking the bottom of my chair and trying to scoot it around with his legs. I'd turn around to confront the goof and the teacher, Mr. Hughes, would tell me in his drill instructor voice to "Face front, soldier." Hughes was also known as "Buffy" outside the classroom for reasons that remained a mystery. I suspected it had something to do with his look, crew cut and a woolly caterpillar of a mustache. His look belonged on the cover of some gay bondage video instead of in front of a chalkboard.

I had my revenge when Monroe would be called on and attempt to stutter an answer. Uh, uh, uh. He couldn't even succeed as a ventriloquist dummy.

At some point, the relationship between Annette and I transformed from being lab partners to, well, we were still trying to figure it out. We were definitely friends, and I was hoping for more. A lot more.

Our class field trip was to the Newport Aquarium. Orm, Annette and I sat in the same seat. Monroe was somewhere in the back with the other hoods and other unfortunates unlucky enough to be trapped there. Orm and I killed time by telling really bad jokes.

Orm. "What do you call a man with no arms and no legs at sea?" "Bob."

My turn. "What's the difference between pizzas and Jews?" "Pizzas don't scream when you put them in an oven."

Orm. "How do you get dead babies out of a truck?" "With a pitchfork."

On and on it went. Annette would shake her head saying that's gross. She laughed the loudest.

At the aquarium, we saw fish I would have loved to have at the other end of my Zebco 33. Good eating too, I bet. It was wild, the color and variety of fish. I'd never seen a real sea horse before. We were lucky enough to see them feed the albino alligator raw chicken too, a far cry from the worms' diet. Annette liked the penguins best. Orm, much like me, seemed fascinated by it all.

The aquarium held two special memories; it was the first time I held Annette's hand. While overlooking the shark tank and staring down into all that water, she suffered a twinge of vertigo. I remember like it was just yesterday, her hand in mine, one hand on my shoulder, her eyes staring into mine, her gag reflex kicking in. One of the attendants screaming, "Not in the tank, not in the tank!"

She didn't puke but had turned so pale she made Orm look tan.

The other memory stood out even more. Annette was wisely hugging the nearest wall outside the eel display. The Moray was almost hidden from view, tucked away in some crevice.

"Hey Orm here's your brother."

Monroe.

Orm stepped forward, one hand on the glass. I could barely hear his words. He turned and smiled.

"Fish have feelings, too."

The eel emerged, a beautiful example of *Gymnomuraena zebra.* The Zebra Moray.

Two feet of scaleless fish swam up to meet the hand. If a fish could smile, this one was grinning, dorsal to anal fin.

"You're a small one," Orm said, returning his hand to his jacket's pocket. "You know, the largest on record gets to be about 10 feet. On record, that is."

I'll never forget the look on his face, like he had a secret and just in knowing that secret, he was content.

The rest of the trip was uneventful, save for some students getting trapped in an elevator, Monroe included. That's what happens when you push all the buttons.

Classes came and went. Homework assigned and completed. Excuses made and signatures forged. New connections established and underage drinkers intoxicated. Summer was drawing closer and both students and teachers were impatient for the school year to end.

I was seeing less of Orm on the weekends and more of Annette. We were still friends but things had changed. Pussy will do that. I was holding more than Annette's hand now. I don't know if I was in love, but I was definitely in love with something.

Hanging around Annette's locker with one more class to go, she was switching books and I was waiting to walk her to class. A large, pockmarked moon eclipsed the aisle.

"When you gonna stop hanging around fags and let me at that snatch? Studs need love too."

Monroe: Always a gentlemen.

Not thinking, I replied, "I thought you preferred heifers, teat sucker. Moooooo."

A pretty good comeback. At least the few students around laughed.

Then I forgot rule Number 7 in the high school survivor guide: If you do make the mistake of insulting the toughest kid in school, don't turn your back.

The warranty on my keep-from-getting-your-ass-kicked detector must have expired. I turned my back.

I don't think anyone got the license plate for the truck that collided with my skull.

He hit me so hard I could smell my breakfast and that was two days old.

I remember waking up on the floor, thinking the circus was in town. After playing soccer with my kidneys, a gorilla wearing size 13s tried to balance himself on my head. I kept wondering if my head would make an audible squish like in the movies.

My life flashed before me. I was still a teenager; it was a short film.

Suddenly, the weight shifted.

Someone said, "That's enough."

It was Orm. He pushed Monroe against the lockers. Monroe was more shocked and off balance than anything. They just stood there staring at each other. Monroe's shirt balled up in Orm's hand, Monroe's meaty arm against Orm's throat. Monroe blinked first. I don't know what was said but Monroe started laughing. It sounded more like a hyena than a human. That's when Orm hit him, faster than a largemouth bass striking a crankbait. Bam. Right in the nose. Monroe started to drip, both from the nose and his eyes. I think he was too shocked in the seconds that followed to retaliate. Then the Buffer stuck his chest between the two and broke things up.

"Gentlemen! Report to the principal's office immediately!"

"Whatever fag," Monroe sniffed.

For the second time that day, Monroe bounced against the lockers.

Both were suspended for fighting. Orm got three days, Monroe a week, since it wasn't his first offense. Mr. Hughes insisted on searching Monroe's locker. No need for probable cause or a search warrant. Wrong community, wrong decade for that type of thing. All that was needed was a bolt cutter.

Some said pot was found, others a gun. Rumors circulated that Hughes planted both. It worked. Monroe was expelled.

A few days later, Orm's hand was still bruised, swollen up like a pufferfish. My face, on the other hand, looked like a drowning victim. I could touch my lips to my nose without even trying, a feat impossible days earlier.

Two weeks to the day of the fight, someone set Orm's hand-me-down Honda on fire. Orm woke to the sound of chickens clucking their heads off and there was his car in flames. It was a piece of shit, the rust holding it together, but it was wheels. The police suspected arson. Even a juggler, his vision lost in a freak accident involving power tools, cheap wine and a midget albino, could have seen that. I had my license, but no car. Annette had both. We gave Orm a lift to and from school.

Monroe would show up in town from time to time, like a booger you can't shake from your finger, "Cow Killer" had been replaced by "Cry Baby," but that was usually only said in unison by groups of at least four. Monroe eventually disappeared. Some said that he ran away to join the Mob, others that Mr. Hughes and his zipper-masked lover needed a new bottom for their twisted games of love. He wasn't missed.

The last week of school, I was having lunch with Orm. Annette was at the Dairy Queen with her friends. Nice enough bunch, but they weren't my type. Too friendly. We went down to the old grand stand to eat. The grand stand was home to a seldom-used baseball diamond. Nobody else there except a few smokers. Orm was always brown bagging his lunch. I had tuna and suggested we swap. My mom knew I hated tuna (it gave me gas), but it still appeared in my lunch from time to time. Orm loved tuna. His lunch consisted of some kind of pasty substance on bread. Like chicken salad.

"What's this?"

"Chicken. Wild chicken. From the farm. Dad killed it last night. It's true what they say about them flopping without their heads. They don't tell you the heads continue to flop. And cluck too. They cluck the future."

"Bullshitter."

It didn't taste like any chicken I'd had before. Salty, like ham. I grinned, wolfing it down. It was delicious. I pulled a small hair from my tongue. What kind of chicken had hair on it?

"One of yours?"

He smiled his typical Orm smile.

"You're right. It's worm food."

"Best worm food I've had."

Orm and his family moved away over the summer. They moved to Houston. "Bigger worms mean bigger profit," as his dad explained. Who could argue?

Annette and I broke up. We lasted three years. No hard feelings. Years later, she was kind enough to autograph a copy of the *Penthouse* she appeared in. She's still my favorite centerfold.

Orm and I stayed in touch for a while. He joined the Navy. I could hardly see him sailing the seas of the world. He used to complain about getting carsick. His ancestor would probably be proud. I just hoped he was happy.

SOMETHING FUNNY IS GOING ON

Journal Entry 14/12

Fuck. Screwed up today. Typical patrol. Eyes and ears open. All senses on the high end of the dial. Body on full alert. Juicing on caffeine and legal stimulants. Weapons cataloged, cleaned and cocked. Not expecting anything but always prepared. Always. I heard laughter. Not the sound of kids playing or schoolgirls with the giggles. This was much heavier, throaty, almost raw. Artificial laughter is one of the telltale signs. We remember. How can we forget the laughter as they killed our friends, our family, our town. You don't forget the hair, the costumes, the frozen smile, death in their lifeless eyes. I was at the Big Top Burger. You don't forget. You don't forgive.

Approached on its blindside. One look at that holly jolly costume, the big boots, the kids drawn in like moths to the flame by that big belly laugh, and I knew my only option. I drew. Five shots at close range. I take no chances. Small entrance, big exit. Always aim for the nose. Feel bad about the kids being blood splattered. Would feel worse if it were their blood. God bless deer slugs and a little American ingenuity. It dropped in mid laugh; its rosy cheeks sucking wind, its belly quivering like Jell-O. The fake beard came off as it fell, struggling for help. But we know they are masters of disguise, mimics without peer. They've got chameleon DNA, reptile instincts. They know how to blend. You've got to be colder, smarter and better than they are. DTA: Don't Trust Anyone. Words to live by.

I remember the bicycle I got on Christmas the year before they came. Mom always loved Christmas. The crusade continues.

Journal Entry 23/12

I hate shoppers. I hate Christmas shoppers. I really hate Christmas shoppers with fucking cell phones. Don't these poor bastards realize their lives are at stake? The shit we could tell them would bug out their color-contact-wearing eyes. They drive around in their gas-guzzling mastodons on wheels with their damn phones surgical attached to their ears just to get a better deal on little Steve's toys. They cut me off three times today. It makes me sick. Well, I've got news for you, buddy; your name's on top of the menu, and it's an all you can eat buffet. Hurry, hurry, step right up. See the non-seeing, non-believing, blind-in-both-eyes, typical American male. Can you say endangered? Fucking cell-phoned, mind-controlled bastards.

Cell phone equals mind control?

Possibility?

Journal Entry 2/1

I wanted to write yesterday, but was still too hung-over. And a happy New Year to you, too.

This time of year is meant to be with family. They took my family away. I was left with only my name, my inheritance and my desire for vengeance. It's been a nightmare merry-go-round ever since.

Sometimes I still can't believe. I understand why so many of the surviving town folk of Crescent Cove refuse to talk about what happened. It's easier to forget. It's easier to pretend they aren't out there. Just look the other way. The government didn't even have to cover up. Self-preservation and the denial factor went into hyper drive. People wanted to talk but they didn't know what to say. The ones that did were locked up and labeled disturbed. Well, Jesus H. Christ, when you see your family cotton candied to death in front of you, I'd say you have the right to be disturbed.

I enlisted to get some answers and learn the art of war. One visit to the hardware store and I've got an arsenal. I can take a guy out five different ways, without him realizing it, without even breaking a sweat. My questions were red-taped from every angle by the top brass on down. It was like Valentines Day. So many sugarcoated responses, so many flat out lies. When I asked the big question, where did all the people go, it was always the same stock answer: People disappear every day. Well, no shit. Why do you think they're disappearing? It's them. They're responsible for more faces on milk cartons than you can imagine.

I feel sorry for the masses. They have no idea. They do the 9 to 5 thing or 8 to 6 thing, or whatever it takes to pay the bills. They have no purpose. They just feed the machine, one way or another. Not me. I know my purpose. I have a mission. I'm a man on a mission. I won't stop. No brakes allowed.

Journal Entry 5/3

I've been traveling, hitting all the little sideshows and amusement parks. There's more than you think. I almost plugged a pair of mimes last week. Their act was so pathetic they had to be human. You can't fake that kind of crap. You never realize how big this country is until you see it from the road. You don't realize how many damn bugs there are either. I could have scrapped them off the windshield using a putty knife. Thick as Mom's mashed potatoes.

I got a tip from one of my contacts. He's a UFO nut who makes a mean pot of chili. He's a news hound. Magazines and newspapers and tapes all over. We don't see eye to eye on many things. I think his theory about Atlantis being covered by the Gobi Desert is a crock. We both agree there's stuff going on that is kept very low on the general public's radar screen. Through the electronic grapevine, he heard about some farmer who found a crop circle in his field. No big deal right. Only the crop circle was in the shape of a smiley face. You don't see the talking faces on the national news networks broadcasting that little factoid, do you? Stick that in your Big Top Burger and see how it tastes.

Journal Entry 6/3

I still have nightmares. Sometimes I dream I'm at the dentist. I'm strapped in, hooked up to the laughing gas. As I'm about to go under, I see this chalk-skinned, pasty-faced monstrosity reach into my mouth with its four-fingered hand and yank out a rubber chicken. The chicken has my mother's face.

I no longer go to movie theatres. The smell of popcorn sickens me.

Journal Entry 8/3

The crop circle was a bust. Damn tourists had trampled the area. Nothing to see. The farmer was still charging admission. Five bucks a pop to see stomped on corn stalks. I guess it beats working. He took my money with a gap-toothed smile. A waste of time this trip, except I did pick up a new laser scope at a gun show. Bang, bang.

Journal Entry 15/3

A bit of a scare today. I thought I was being followed by one of those damn Mini Cooper cars. Damn things look like toys. Turned out to be some young blond more interested in applying mascara than chasing my ass. Too bad, as she was very pretty. She can tailgate me anytime. Still, you can never be too careful. We know they prefer compact cars.

Journal Entry 3/5

I haven't had much time to write. I needed to re-group, rethink my mission. Some fucker stole my note-book. Years' worth of notes in some idiot's hands. He probably just threw it away. A blueprint for survival gone just like that.

But there is a ray of sunshine. I was having breakfast when the notebook was stolen. I went to the bathroom and then… poof. Gone. But my eggs were still there. So was the local newspaper. The headline said a new fast food joint was opening tomorrow. It's going to be the biggest in the area, complete with an indoor/outdoor playground. There's going to be prizes and a costume contest. Hell, there's even going to be a parade. They love parades. It's like candy. The occasion doesn't mat-ter. I've seen them at St Patrick's and Opening Days. They can't resist.

Since Crescent Cove, they are subtler. They don't display themselves openly. They've gotten better at passing as human. That's why I didn't realize it before. All this time it was staring at me in the face.

I'll be at the opening.

Journal Entry 4/5

Today is the day. I'm ready. Everything is cataloged, cleaned and cocked.

To beat your enemy, you have to become your enemy. Crescent Cove haunts me. I will never have a normal life until they are extinct. I know this as I apply the pancake make up. I fluff out the multi-colored curls of my wig. I pull on the mismatched golf trousers I picked up at a thrift store. The oversized shoes I'll put on when I'm there. It's humanly impossible to drive wearing them.

I imagine what it will be like, the laser scope targeting the face, one trigger away from making the red nose even redder, white stained crimson.

I hope there is a gaggle of them.

I have a mission. I have a destination.

The Golden Arches. Today and every day after.

WATER'S EDGE

Everett was bored. So far, this trip had been a bust. All he had gotten was sunburn, bug bites, dirty looks from his fellow female tourists, firm rebukes by the local wenches. The hole in his bank account kept getting bigger; these oversea trips weren't cheap. He was here to have sex, cash checks and not worry about the after effects.

To top things off, last night's dinner was waging war with today's breakfast. He dreaded picking a winner. His sphincter felt unreliable, like a dragonfly was buzzing between his butt cheeks and he was afraid to set it free.

What a day!

The drone of the guide's voice didn't help. After she had turned down his dinner offer, he had tuned her out. She looked so smug in her mirrored sunglasses, tight brown shorts and too-cute freckles. He still wondered if the freckles trailed to her voluptuous chest but not so much after the third rejection. Everett thought she didn't know what she was talking about. Hadn't she just said no crocodiles had been seen in these parts in decades?

What a load of wallaby shit.

He'd watched enough National Geographic programs as a kid to know the difference between a common lizard and a croc. There was no mistaking the flat snout, the fearsome saw-blade jaws that would grow more dangerous with age. There were about a dozen of the little buggers right there, babies about eight inches in length, floating above that sunken log.

Dumb bitch, he thought to himself, kneeling down to get a better look.

The log, eyes protected by nictitating membranes and fully alert, watched and slowly moved closer.

GodTV

Bob isn't a nice guy. He isn't the type to go around kicking dogs or sucker punching women. He's never shot, stabbed, or blown someone up courtesy of a homemade bomb or retail explosive. Such methods of murder are messy in more ways than one. Fingerprints, bloodstains, and headlines invite trouble. They are the dreams of little minds. Bob prides himself on being a thinker, a dreamer. He is patient. He takes his time. Bob isn't a nice guy but it's not something he broadcasts.

As a senior in high school, Bob dated a girl named Tonya. She was a junior and new in town. Her parents moved to Rushville over the summer. Bob and Tonya met at the local animal shelter. Tonya and her family were looking for a new pet. Bob worked at the shelter part-time. He introduced the family to Shelby, a plump, lovable cat, full of fun and mischief. He introduced himself to Tonya.

It was a short romance, as high-school romances tend to be. Tonya ended the relationship rather abruptly, saying she wanted to date other people. She hoped they could remain friends. Bob took the news amazingly well, hugged Tonya one final time, and hoped for her happiness. Tonya dated one of the more popular athletes. Bob always smiled when he saw them together.

Chameleons are the fashion plates of the reptile world, capable of changing their skin pigment. This camouflage ability helps these slow moving creatures survive. They blend with their surroundings. Color changes can range from green, brown, yellow, combinations of colors and even black. As amazing as these creatures are, even they would have been jealous of Bob's smile, the sincerity of it, the razors it concealed.

Three months following the breakup, Shelby went missing. Flyers didn't help nor did the offered reward. Tonya and her parents were heartbroken. The family loved that cat. Even Bob was saddened. Shelby was a great cat and it wasn't the feline's fault Tonya was such a cold bitch. Bob felt bad as he raised the hammer. But it didn't stop the hammer from falling. And falling.

Bob was there the day Tonya's dad discovered what was left of Shelby, recognizable only by his tag. He watched, courtesy of his binoculars, as Shelby was dumped in the trashcan. Bob had to dig the damn cat out and placed the body behind the front tire of Tonya's Toyota. Bob loved reunions and wanted to make sure Tonya didn't miss this one.

Another girlfriend, later in college, also broke Bob's heart. Lisa, an accounting major, told Bob she was breaking up with him because, quite honestly, she couldn't stand him. She called him a control freak, a gossipy little bitch, pathetic in bed and numerous other things all in front of those gathered at the Student Union. Bob took it all in stride, never shedding a tear or lowering himself to Lisa's level. He was above it, certainly above her and the other gawking students.

That December, Lisa went home for Christmas. It was her favorite time of year. Her family went all out:

lawn decorations, a huge meal with all the trimmings and a gift exchange to make Santa blush. Lisa was opening one of her presents, a lavishly decorated box featuring snowmen frolicking, topped with a huge red bow. She was having trouble with the contents when a large brownish lump fell onto her lap.

The lump, all nine inches of it, was *Theraphosa blondi* better known as the Goliath Tarantula. Like most tarantulas whose bite is non-lethal to human, Lisa's surprise Christmas gift would have been fine had she not started screaming and flicking at the thing. The bird eater, when agitated and it certainly was with all that noise, is capable of flicking its own body hair through the air at the perceived threat. In this case, Lisa was the target. The tiny hairs are extremely irritating especially if they contact the eyes and mouth. Poor Lisa got a face full and failed to return to school that semester as she proved to be hyper allergic. The nightmares persisted long after her health returned to normal.

It's funny the things you remember about certain people, like their middle names, their choice of perfume or the car they drive. The thing in Bob's memory that stood out the most about Lisa, aside from her dumping him, was that she suffered from arachnophobia, fear of spiders.

Bob isn't a nice guy. He has proven that over the years. Numerous little things like making prank phone calls, keying cars, breaking windows, sugaring fuel tanks, subscribing people to magazines they don't want, damaging credit profiles, ruining marriages and lives all in the name of revenge. Little things that have shaped his life.

Today, Bob makes his living as a tabloid columnist. He is hated, despised, but read by thousands. His targets: the gods that live among us. You've seen them. On

TV, the movies, their tell-all books, magazines. Indeed, how can you avoid seeing them? Bob shows us the dirt beneath their nails, the drunken outbursts, the illegitimate kids, the addictions, the little things that enrich so many lives. Bob makes them human. He brings them down and delights in doing it, even if their careers and lives suffer. Bob sees himself as an assassin, words his weapon. It's a dirty job but necessary. Although he hasn't won any awards for his efforts and in the past has been spit on, threatened and even physically accosted, the result of which led to an out of court settlement, Bob is a wealthy man with legions of readers.

So when the doorbell to his condo rang, although surprised, he was not completely taken off guard. Bob tried to keep a certain degree of anonymity. His phone number was unlisted. His column's byline was Robert Glitz, a far cry from the Bob Van Hinkle that grew up in the Midwest. However, the occasional fan did show up on his doorstep, usually the president of whoever's hot this month fan club wanting insider dirt. Sometimes a celebrity, almost forgotten, wanting their name in the headlines again, regardless of how they might be painted. Or one who was pissed off at something he wrote and wanted their pound of flesh. But that was only on the rarest of occasions.

Bob crept to the peephole, a nine iron within easy reach just in case. At the peephole, he saw the whitest teeth he had ever seen, a shark's smile. Behind that smile, a face permanently tanned, so lobster red it looked painful. With a wink, the face said "Avon calling."

Bob didn't like being disturbed, unless it was by some wannabe starlet with prefab tits. "Who the fuck are you", Bob retorted. "I don't remember ordering Chinese, pizza or asshole."

The face muttered something to a figure standing behind him.

"I didn't hear that. Come again?" Bob asked, the nine iron now in hand.

The face again, "What I said was I tried it the easy way, smart guy."

The face rapped hard on the door. Once, twice, three times, followed by a blinding flash then darkness, thick as chocolate pudding.

Bob came to, feeling not only like he had the mother of all hangovers come to visit but also invited all her illegitimate children. He felt like shit. What the hell had happened? He remembered teeth—perfect, even by Hollywood standards.

Then the voice behind the teeth introduced himself.

"Welcome back, Mr. Congeniality. My business associate and I were just discussing your fashion sense. How exactly would you describe the color of these drapes? The only word that springs to mind is diarrhea. And the wallpaper. Did the Institute for the Blind have some kind of interior design demonstration? I've seen better patterns in stepped-in dog shit, I gotta tell you buddy. By the by, the name's Archie…" The voice finally paused, "and that lump of humanity over there is… well, you can call him Lump. He won't mind. Promise."

Still groggy, Bob tried to pay attention to his uninvited guests. His eyes drifted towards his hands. He couldn't move; garbage bags tied around his wrists, elbows, knees and ankles restricted his movement. He didn't recognize either stranger. This Archie was a talker, a game show host or politician in the making, and his partner was one big motherfucker. Bob also realized, most importantly, this had the makings of a really bad day.

Archie dressed as loudly as he spoke. A peach col-ored sport coat and beneath that a shirt decorated with various types of peppers. His pants matched the coat. A wardrobe like his would get your ass beat in the wrong bar but Archie had the type of face that welcomed the threat of violence. His curly hair was an unnatural red, like tiny flames dancing on his skull. His partner was decked out all in black: jacket, slacks, shades, motorcy-cle boots and sock hat, obscuring most of his face. Good thing, too, because he was the *U* in *Ugly*. He looked like a shaved ape turned gangsta. The temperature had to be pushing 90 outside and this dude looked like he could sweat ice cubes.

"What the fuck…" Bob started only to be cut off.

"Sorry about the inconvenience but politeness and five bucks will get you a hand job. You want a hand job from him? I thought not. Lump and myself are free-lancers. We're working stiffs with bills to pay. Com-prende? I've read your column in that rag. Bob Glitz right? Complete crap but my taste runs more towards *Dear Annie* or those old crime magazines with stories like *Welcome to puberty, Pamela… I'm your Rapist* or *The Slaugh-tered Nudes of Horror House.* Remember those? No ac-counting for tastes. So who am I to judge, right?"

Archie stood and pointed at something hanging on the wall. It was a velvet painting of O.J. Simpson, wear-ing an apron that once read, "Kiss the Cook." Only it had been graffitied over. It now read, "Kill the Crook."

"That I like," Archie indicated to Lump.

Struggling against the knots without success, Bob be-gan to laugh. "This is a joke right. Some kind of practi-cal joke. Did Samantha hire you? It had to be one of those fucks at the office. Or better yet, this is some new TV show. Where's the camera? Reality shows are get-ting all the ratings. What's the name of this one? I got it… *Captured* or *Home Invasion*. It's gonna be called *Ten to Twenty* if you bastards don't untie me. Right. Now."

Archie lit a cigarette, "You are a funny guy, you know. Feisty too. I might have been wrong about you. Let's play pretend. A game show, right? You, my friend, are on GodTV. This is the pilot, the very first episode. Make us proud. Our target audience is all the revenge minded bible bangers out there but we figure it will have loads of crossover appeal. Everybody's got a beef with somebody right. We plan on doing huge numbers, especially in the South and in Europe. You know *Sinners in the Hands of an Angry God* type stuff. You're playing the part of the sinner. It's like *Candid Camera* on crack."

"Sounds like a hit. So what are you guys? Angles with attitude? The most menacing thing about you is your shirt. Now will you please untie me before any lawyers have to get involved," pleaded Bob. "And please, put that cigarette out. I have allergies."

Archie stubbed the cigarette against his hand and paced the room. "No problem. Your wish, my command, right. Angels? No, we're no glory boys, sissies with golden wings. We're not afraid to get our hands dirty if you know what I mean."

Bob's stomach growled. He had not eaten anything today except a slice of leftover pizza. Archie's sizzling hand had the odor of bacon.

Archie walked past Lump. So far the big fellow hadn't said a word, not even a grunt, just stood there with his sunglasses, looking big.

"Here's the scenario, Bob. You don't mind if I call you Bob, do you? Course not. We're still playing pretend. Let's say there was this girl, no names. Protect the guilty and avoid the lawsuit, right. There's this girl, pretty young thing, a rising star in the Hollywood sky, who you mentioned in that compost heap you call a column. Sound familiar?"

Bob shook his head. Chicks were bought by the pound in this town. Step on the scale and take off your cloths. Don't care to play, hop the bus back to Kansas. It's just business, pure and simple.

"Don't recall? Course not, no reason why you should. A dime a dozen, right? You had some pretty bad things to say but that's your game right. So what if you made up the crap about her junkie porn star past. If it's in print, it has to be true, right? Seeing is believing."

Archie pulled out another cigarette but failed to light it. "Bob, you're a popular guy. Nationwide circulation, am I right? Get this. Her mom reads the article. Her mom. The girl tries to call home but mom in tears refuses to take her calls, saying she doesn't have a daughter. You get what I'm saying. Now every casting call she goes to she's expected to deliver if you know what I mean. As a result of your column, every skin company in town is calling her, offering her a job. But those are the only parts she's offered."

"I don't understand," Bob whined. "Sounds like I did her a favor. What's this got to do with me? Who are you guys? Where's your film crew. I haven't signed any kind of release. I'm gonna fucking kill Samantha. I'll double what she's paying you. What's she paying you?"

"Patience. By the balls of Christ, it's hot in here," Archie said, wiping his brow and removing his coat. "Too cheap for AC? The heat I can take; the humidity is another story. Go to Heaven for the climate, Hell for the company. That's what Pops use to say."

Archie handed his coat to Lump, who tossed it over a chair.

"As I was saying, this girl, she's the real emotional type right. She doesn't know what to do. She's been all but blacklisted. Nobody wants to hear her side of the story. Not the press. Not her family. Guess what happens? She gets hit by a fucking bus. A tour bus, the kind you take to see where the famous croaked. Guess she's part of the tour now, right. She didn't see the damn thing coming. Blinded by her tears. Tragic. Messed up so bad, it was a closed casket. If that's not a movie of the week, I don't know what is."

Bob twisted in his restraints, feeling more and more like an ant under the magnifying glass. "Not a bad story. A little bit of drama, a touch of tragedy. What you need is a writer. I can put you in touch with the best. I know this guy, he use to be a speechwriter for the governor. He can spin better than any DJ. This guy is guaranteed gold with a capital dollar sign."

Archie winked at Lump. "What do you think? 'Tragedy,' he says."

The big man's lips moved slightly. On anyone else, it might have made a poor, but passable smile. On Lump, the facial gesture would have scared small children. Lump slowly peeled off his leather jacket. Beneath, he was shirtless and heavily tattooed, some kind of weird tribal design. It looked painful and expensive. Lump's chest was big enough to pass for a missing continent.

"You doing ok, Lump?" Archie asked. "Lump's not what you would call a chatter box. He's the strong silent type, emphasis on strong. Me, I can't shut up. It's the Pentecostal in me. But I digress. Rumor has it that you knew this little filly, Bob. Dated her a couple times. Had a rather public yelling match over at that restaurant on Madison. Any truth to that? Her name was Bonnie."

Bob remembered Bonnie. How could he forget? Her hair the color of sunflowers, 32-inch legs made even longer in those red fuck-me pumps, her corn-fed midwestern naïveté. He liked Bonnie; she reminded him of the small town he grew up in. And left as soon as he got the chance. He remembered, promising her the world just to climb between her thighs. Prom queen pussy. Once she delivered, well… Bob liked to think of himself as the welcome wagon for all the new Hollywood wannabes and this wannabe had unfortunately worn out her welcome. Bob swore he would never let another woman (or man) get the better of him. Not after everything he had done to grasp the golden ring. So far, he'd been true to his word, one of the few times.

"Look guys, fun's fun but I really have to get going," Bob stammered. "I've got places to be, people to see. I'll have my people call your people and we can talk numbers and percentages. I date a lot a people. It's a job perk. You can't hold me responsible for this girl's tragic accident. Who set this up? Untie me, and we can forget all about this. I can get you guys a lot of free publicity."

"You know you're right, Bob. We don't hold you responsible so it's nothing personal. Unfortunately, the girl's father does." Archie blew a smoke ring in the form of a mushroom cloud. "Her old man has connections if you know what I mean. When he heard the news, he went cashews. Once he got a grip, he pieced together his daughter's last days. Did you know she kept a diary? She mentioned you by name. Calls were made, old favors called in, deals cut, sacrifices bled, contracts signed. You understand. It's just business."

Archie disposed of his cigarette and rolled up his sleeves, revealing horrible burns. "Gasoline can do funny things to your flesh. I was putting the finishing touches on this family. Mom, Dad, two kids and was torching the bodies when the flames turned traitor. Course, this is nothing compared to what happened later. At the courthouse, a pissed-off relative shot my cock off. Those stupid fucks let me bleed to death on the steps."

Archie dropped his pants. "Not pretty is it? You think I want to spend eternity like this? No way in hell. Which brings us to why we're here."

Lump stepped forward, twisting his neck like it needed to be cracked.

"You can consider us God's wrath. Hard to believe a boy from small-town Alabama would be doing the Lord's work. But the way I see it, we're all just part of His puzzle, doing what we can to fit in. Lump here is from Egypt originally. Fourth Dynasty. That's right: camels and sand and all that shit. He tortured people for a living and let me tell you, those Egyptians made it an art form. Not a bad living. I did it for free, but Lump was a professional, until the Pharaoh Khafre caught Lump making time with one of his mistresses."

Archie pointed at Lump's immense chest. "These tattoos are actually hieroglyphs. They serve as binding spells. The Pharaoh had his priests inscribe this chicken scratch all over Lump's body, right? The Pharaoh's mistress had her eyes burned from their sockets. I think she wound up as a base of a pyramid. A little Jimmy Hoffa humor. But Lump… he was made an example of. Those Egyptians didn't take death or payback lightly."

"This can't be happening." Bob struggled against his bonds. "This can't be real."

"You know that's what I said when I first got to the lower H." The shark's grin was back. "Eternity is a hell of a long time, know what I mean. I decided to make the best of it. Lump and myself used to be what in Hell is known as Disciplinarians, Kind of like guidance counselors for the Damned. We helped recent transfers come to terms with the situation they found themselves in. We did such a good job we were promoted. Now we're in Retribution. I'm the mouth and he's the muscle. It works out pretty well."

Archie ran a hand through his hair. It came away dripping.

"Never would have guessed I'm a natural blond." He flicked the liquid from his fingers onto Bob. "The blood of innocents."

The room was filled with a rustling noise, like fallen leaves blown across the grave.

Archie continued. "The Pharaoh was righteously pissed. Ever hear of dermestids? It's a type of bug, beetle actually. Those Egyptians loved their animals. Their gods had the heads of jackals and crocodiles. Blasphemy, I know, but what do you expect from a bunch of heathens. No offence, Lump. Anyway these beetles, what an Einsteiner like you might call a scarab, were sacred. Me, I come from a long line of snake handlers and I can't stand the damned things. If you can't grill it, forget it. My point being scarabs were sacred. They symbolized immortality. They ate things, too."

Bob was sweating in places he didn't know he could sweat. When this was all over, he was definitely going to sue the shit out of somebody, guaran-goddamn-teed. The rustling sound grew louder.

Archie stared at Lump. "These beetles are used in museums today. That's how they get their specimen skeletons so clean. You got to be careful though cause they can eat through linoleum, steel, glass, even concrete. Now just imagine what they could do to a former head torturer with a hard-on for serving girls? Damn things love the smell of blood. When the priests were finished carving the hieroglyphs into Lump's skin, the poor bastard looked like a crossword puzzle. The kicker was the hieroglyphs made sure the bugs stayed in place. What I'm saying is the Pharaoh set it up so Lump was going to be eaten alive from the inside out for eternity. And they say life's a bitch."

Bob shook his head. This had to be a joke. In the history of pranks, this was going down as one of the all-time best. If his hands were free, he would salute the sheer genius of it, that is, right after he had pulled the unmarked pistol from his bedroom drawer and shut these guys up permanently.

Archie continued to flick blood at Bob.

"Of course, things have a way of changing when you hit the lower H. The Boss has a sick sense of humor and his boss, well, you can never be too sure now can you? I mean, just look at us."

Archie winked. "You'll see what I mean soon enough."

"Lump, it's time for your close-up. Show me that smile, the one that makes women drip and men flip. You-know-who might be watching."

Lump leaned forward, his flesh rippling, the hieroglyphs becoming animated.

"This one's for Bonnie."

Lump opened his mouth unnaturally wide and vomited darkness.

Bob managed to scream before the first beetle landed on his face. More beetles and screams quickly followed.

*   *   *

The scarabs finished Bob in less than 12 hours.

"Hungry buggers. Looks like I owe you dinner again."

Lump shrugged his massive shoulders and offered Archie a stick of gum. Trident. Archie stuck the gum in his mouth, flicked off the lights and closed the door.

The two demons, their job now finished, walked out into the city of dreams.

ROT & ROLL

Lenny, like disco, was dead. Being dead was new to him. It was like trying on a leather jacket for the first time: you had to get use to the feel of the leather, the new sensations, how your body moved in it. You had to try it out, see how it fit, snug but not too snug. Most importantly, how cool did it make you look? Lenny's death wasn't cool at all.

He was the victim of a car accident. It was a minor fender bender, nothing a couple hundred bucks couldn't fix. A shiny, blue BMW rear-ended a sticker-in-the-window-new SUV. Happens all the time, every day in every city. Nothing to blow your brains out or slit your wrists over. Lenny wasn't even driving, just watching.

But when the midget tumbled out of the SUV and started kicking Mr. Businessman right above the ankle and cursing like a ghetto-born witch turned rap star, Lenny couldn't stop laughing. You could have told him he was being charged with pedaling child porn and would be spending the next several years of his life playing spouse to an assortment of gentlemen so well endowed, the word "freak" could only be used in the most complimentary fashion and his guffaws still would not have ceased. Lenny could not help himself. He was overcome by the physical comedy complete with expletive driven soundtrack being played out before him.

It was hilarious, better than one of those wacky home videos showing some guy getting hit in the nuts or a clown sex orgy or even someone with Tourette's Syndrome turned bonfire.

Lenny thought it was a midget and not a dwarf because the little guy wasn't wearing chain mail or a beard or wielding a battle-axe. Lenny didn't believe in hobbits. He has seen a reality show on dwarves; they were real. It was those little legs in motion that made him bust a gut. They couldn't actually be hurting the suit-and-tie dude. No way. The kicks lacked momentum, no power to their pop. The *GQ* giant bent over to calm his aggressor down and the dwarf went all Thorin Oakenshield on his too-tall ass, pushing him down to street level. When the little guy gave the dude a mini stink face, sticking his munchkin butt right in the guy's nose, Lenny lost it. He started choking on the meatball sub he was eating. Tomato sauce dripped down his chin onto his shirt, making him look like some vampire slob. Swiss cheese snotted out his left nostril. He was turning a lovely shade of cyan and no one was paying him or his now Marty Feldman-like eyes any attention.

The police were already in route due to the accident. Cops were cuffing the BMW owner, hair still immaculate and tie only slightly askew. The midget was being treated for his injures after being used as a broom once Mr. Businessman regained his composure. He had grabbed the midget by his still-kicking legs and started sweeping the pavement. The EMTs were busy picking asphalt out of the little guy's face. When they eventually noticed Lenny lying prone like a wrestler set to take a Jimmy "Superfly" Snuka splash, it was too late. Lenny received a blanket, shielding his face from the summer sun; not that he needed it. He was already dead. Death by sandwich.

But his end was just a beginning. Lenny was a deceased who had failed to cease. He had been recycled, and as someone concerned with the environment, Lenny was cool with that. Green was definitely an "in" thing, and Lenny had always been hip to what was hip. He considered the change to his complexion an improvement.

Lenny wasn't the only one who had been recycled. Some people took offense at seeing the dead walk. Others took baseball bats, golf clubs and other sports equipment and created new games. Cornhole had given way to Between the Eyes as the new weekend pastime. Plant the Machete was popular, too, until a chunk of flesh was lost, the penalty of getting too close. Death, it seemed, could really work up an appetite and there were no vegetarians among the recently lifeless. Even lawn darts made a comeback with a small revision: Now, the goal was to stick the lawn dart *in* someone's eye

Paranoia set in faster than maggots on road kill. People didn't know what the hell to think, although several evangelists swore that was the cause. God's wrath, voodoo terrorism, Mother Earth PMSing, and an alien takeover were all possible explanations for the dead stumbling and bumbling about.

Some blamed the government. The government's official response was "no comment." That and "run" when the White House became the Red House after the dead arrived on the front lawn. Bleeding-heart liberal took on a new meaning, but they weren't the only ones bleeding. One Republican rally looked like a Hollywood premiere, squishy red carpet and all.

Lenny didn't have time for games or explanations; he woke up in the grocery store freezer right behind the bottled beer (the morgues were already too crowded) and next to a girl whose face looked like it had French kissed the business end of a lawnmower. Nice tits though. He felt a jolt through his system, like he had pissed on a lawnmower spark plug. Lenny had heard stuff on the news about the dead walking. He didn't pay it much heed. *They* were always trying to scare the little guy. Fear was better than coupons for making people rich. He had heard that message in a thousand songs a thousand times. That reminded him: Lenny had places to be.

Before his untimely demise, he had purchased a ticket for the upcoming Crib Death concert. He had all their CDs, knew all the lyrics. He even had their "Slut from Sodom" single, limited to a pressing of 666 copies. Damned if he was missing the show. Nothing barring an invitation to a necrophiliac party of buxom play-mates from DropDeadGoregous.com would keep him from the show. And maybe not even that.

Both feet were asleep. His entire body felt like it was asleep. All pins and needles. But lack of circulation could do that to a person. He lumbered out of the grocery store, cold cans of PBR in even colder hands, and headed for home.

For a five-time divorcee, part-time lingerie store manager and full-time floozy, Lenny's mom had her good points; most notably she spent more time at the neighborhood bar than nosing in his business. Lenny prayed she hadn't had time to snoop through his draw-ers or worse, sell his stuff at a garage sale. Hopefully, his stash of pot would be where he left it and, more impor-tantly, the concert ticket.

His house key along with his wallet had gone missing prior to his arrival at the grocery store. Luckily, Lenny remembered the hidden key under the Go Away doormat. He bought the mat at the mall a few years ago. His mom even liked it. He wondered how his mom would react to his present condition. Probably how she reacted to everything. The gin and tonic solution: heavy on the gin, easy on the tonic.

His dope and the ticket were right where he left them. The ticket in his underwear drawer and the dope stuffed inside a Don Post Vampire mask on his bookshelf. Mom wasn't around, no doubt drowning her sorrows over her only son's death.

A dog had taken a liking and a licking to him on the way home. Lenny had always liked dogs. He stopped to pet the stray and had a nice gash to show for it. The dog, hungry for any kind of scraps, had chomped on Lenny's right hand. He was always a champion coagulator and zombification hadn't changed a thing. Not a drop of blood. But he didn't have time to play chew toy.

Lenny duct taped the wound. He fired up the joint and combed his hair with swollen fingers. Maybe he would meet some babes tonight who liked their men jaundiced, stiff and decayed. Dying had done wonders for his acne, too. His zits just flaked off. He just had to be careful that too much of his face wasn't removed in the picking process.

Lenny looted his mom's Elvis cookie jar to get enough change for the bus.

While waiting, he saw a few others doing the Frankenstein shuffle. Nobody paid him much attention but that had always been the case. In the classroom, it was like he had never-call-on-me camouflage and it worked. Unfortunately, it worked not only on teachers and would-be bullies, but also on chicks. Lenny never had much luck with the ladies. Too shy.

The bus arrived. Groomed and exhumed, he dropped his 75 cents in the machine. The bus was mostly empty just some weekend shoppers and shopping mall gangstas with their gold-plated grills. Lenny took a seat in the middle where he didn't have to listen to the hip-hop horror coming from the rap fan's earphones. That's a sure way to get hemorrhoids in your auditory canal, Lenny thought somewhere in the R complex of his brain.

He hadn't even gotten slightly high from the pot. Death could be a real buzzkill. The smoke did seem to eliminate most of the bugs that had been haloing his head though. Someone had graffitied "Dead People are Cool" on the seat. Lenny smiled a rigor grin.

By the time Lenny arrived at the venue, the show had already started, which wasn't necessarily a bad thing because he hated lines. It was intermission. Lenny found an open spot on the wall and squished against it.

Inside was a gathering of tribes. Punks, skinheads, skaters, goths, headbangers, posers. It looked like the ugly parade had ended its route here. There was more black mascara and white make up than at a mime convention.

Lenny fit right in.

They were all there for one reason: To see Crib Death, to hear their music. OK, that's two reasons.

Lenny watched two guys sporting tattoos and matching bad mustaches, eyeballing every female that came into view. They were like human vultures with peach fuzz. All part of the food chain. The pot might not have gotten him high, but he had a killer case of the munchies.

The lights went out. A sole spotlight illuminated a huge banner glowing in florescent red, a drawing of a fetus with horns. It was Crib Death's logo. Lenny had a matching design on his shirt. The solidified tomato sauce gave it a surreal look.

The crowd grew thicker as he neared the stage. From the shadows stepped Crib Death. The crowd roared its enthusiasm, like spectators at the Colosseum cheering for the lions.

What the hell? Lenny couldn't believe his unblinking eyes. That wasn't Steve (S.S.) Steel on the mike. And that intro music—that wasn't the guitar riff to "Jesus Christ Scarecrow." It made the worst rap album sound good. It was like a pitchfork against a chalkboard, which would usually sound cool as hell. But this was like a fifth grade Music Ed class for the mentally challenged.

If Satan ever gave up his job as tormentor of mankind and got a gig as a musician, Crib Death would be his band. They were that kind of heavy. You could invade countries on the strength of their ballads. The stuff coming out of the speakers should have been going down a commode.

This…this was EMO. Music for Sesame Street, not Elm Street. You close your eyes, try to get some eternal peace and the world goes to hell in a Hello Kitty handbag. Lenny wasn't recycled for this. He made for the stage, one lurching step at a time.

Bodies battered him. Human shrapnel from the mosh pit, proving the theory if a tree falls in the woods, sound or no sound, you can always mosh. Lenny kept walking. His chest absorbed an assortment of elbows, his toes were stomped and a bottle bounced off his head. Lenny didn't feel a thing. He was on a mission.

The crowd surged. Lenny was like a hamburger wrapper in the wind. Fingers sank into his flesh like it was stale cheese. He didn't care. He surfed the sea of hands until he was on stage.

Eel Edmuds was on lead guitar. Bob Hackenmeister was battering his custom pentagram bass. The other original members were accounted for so who was this Nancy boy posing as their singer. No way. The joker was wearing a sweater and matching scarf.

Lenny had no way of knowing Steve (S.S.) Steel, the voice of Crib Death had died just days before his own death. A bitter combination of GBH and fat girl snatch proved to be his undoing. A Fender to the back of the skull put S.S. down for the second and final time. Death by guitar. It seemed all too fitting.

Lenny had no way of knowing the new crooner, Antonio Samuel Scott Jr., was the manager's nephew. A lot of strings had been pulled—most notably the manager's strings by his wife—to get Antonio the spot. She had begged and pleaded, offered plenty of oral and finally threatened. It was the "D" word that finally did it. Not death or decapitation or dismemberment but divorce. The manger's wallet conceded. Antonio wasn't without talent and ambition. He could carry a tune and his greatest unfulfilled rock star ambition was to appear on *American Idol*. He was about as Heavy Metal as tinfoil.

Lenny did know this tool was wearing a shirt with a collar, and there wasn't anything metal about wearing a shirt with a collar. Unless it was studded.

♫ *I need a friend, one I can trust and love and hug.* ♫

Lenny cut the annoying sound off at the source.

The sissy singer's throat was as red as Satan's asshole. His last notes stained the crowd, stained Lenny.

Security didn't know what to do. The band, instruments limp in their hands, stared at each other, stared at Lenny.

The crowd went wild.

Lenny ate it up, swallowed, digested. He had never felt so alive. With a sloth's grace, he picked up the mike. And launched into his favorite Crib Death song: "A Lullaby for Lazaus." The band paused, picked up the crowd's reaction and let it rip. Guitars screamed echoing the crowd.

Lenny sounded like he had been fellatiating cutlery. It was the sound of the dammed, the depressed, the dead. It was his sound. It was their sound. He was now lead growler, a position he would have died for. And did.

The crowd loved it.

The band rocked on.

DRAGON SKIN

The skull grinned down at him like an emaciated jester. Forged steel split bone in one fluid motion. Kruth didn't get the joke. He grasped the skull while sheathing his sword. The gap-toothed grin suggested a happy death, but the splintered hole above the right eye socket suggested otherwise. A mallet, mace, or some other massive force had splintered the skull. Death was instant. The skull appeared human; no demon had teeth that yellowed from decay. This was the 20th boneman he had passed. Not even enough flesh left to feed the crows. He stared into the empty eye socket as if the skull would reveal more mysteries. Kruth was no necromancer, had no patience with corpses; he was a warrior, a mercenary, a thief. The secrets of the dead belonged to the dead and his sword arm would never pry their secrets from them. He tossed the skull over his muscled shoulder, the lower jaw cracking on impact, just more debris left in his wake.

Kruth wiped the sweat from his brow. Days like this he often pondered what his life would have been like had he followed his father's profession as a barkeep. Good drink and fair maidens, true, but no adventure, just hearing tales of others instead of living them.

Still, a full glass and fuller bosom may have been the better offer. Instead, Kruth was on a mission for the

God-King, Tyrannis. Tyrannis had promised him the hand of one of his daughters, the fair Symbrosa. Kruth had already acquainted himself with her hand as well as the rest of her anatomy the night before he began this mission. He could recall her heaving, freckled breasts, her skin so smooth from a life of royal comfort, like woven silk it was. He wondered if her bruises had faded and if she longed for new ones. Royalty or not, Kruth treated all woman for what they were, instruments for his pleasure. Was he not known by the white-bearded barbarians to the north as the *Ram's Head* for his prowess in the bedchamber? It wasn't solely for the war-helm he favored on the battlefield, that's for certain.

Tyrannis had also promised Kruth a military position, one commanding a division of the royal army. Kruth wondered if the saying was true: *Heavy is the head that wears the crown.* Perhaps he would find out and trade in his war helm for one made of gold. His sword had cleaved many a head from its shoulders, relieving the weight and demands of life. He saw it as a gift, a small sacrifice in a single stroke, one that typically benefited him. Kruth had his own saying: *heavy is the hand that carries the head.* Tyrannis himself had seized the throne in a military coup. But that was the future. Let the Whores of Fate sort it out. Better to concentrate on the mission at hand.

The mission was one of diplomacy. Tyrannis hoped to open trade with the lands to the East. Such trade would fill the royal coffers and Tyrannis was always looking to expand his rule. The problem was the trade routes traveled through the Valley of Shadows. The slant-eyed Easterners were afraid to commit to the agreement in fear of He-Who-Must-Not-Be-Named, the Shadow Walker, the Forgotten One, His Royal Personage in Black.

Tyrannis told Kruth of the myths, tales of the legend that walked the world without leaving footprints, whose voice caused the Earth to tremble. Tyrannis scoffed at the stories, thinking of them as old wives tales meant to scare children. But the Easterners refused to barter. Tyrannis could not ignore the fear in their voice.

There would be no trade without the Shadow Walker's consent.

Or his head.

Tyrannis had already dispatched messengers of peace to the Valley of Shadows. None had returned. A regiment of soldiers had followed and also gone missing.

Kruth knew that many lips that had voiced promises of peace had been squeezed from a throat held in an iron vice or with a dagger pointed at its back. Brute force overcame the failure of polite politics and feigned diplomacy every time. Kruth, however, was an ambassador of death. He was well suited for the position. He had fought in the Pain Pits of Skarvania, warred with many a wizard and their whelp, and for every scar he bore (and he had several) he had sent twelve fold to a premature and much deserved death. None barred his path and lived. The bodies dispatched in his path served as footnote to his growing legend. Tyrannis had heard the legend and sought out Kruth's aid. Tyrannis was a politician and knew it was better to have a sword at your side than threatening to spill your entrails from behind.

Kruth had heard tales of this Forgotten One, in taverns and back alleys, in hushed breath. It was said he was a man who moved as fast as a serpent, a death strike at the touch of his hands. Whispers said he was a life stealer in a single motion, a fighter of unparalleled skill, that he was the greatest combatant on two legs. Some said he stood eye-to-eye with giants while others whispered that he was withered as a crone, bent by the black sin coursing in his veins. Dealings with the Dark Arts had rendered him all but a cripple. He had traded his physical form for spells capable of incinerating a man in his boots, before a sword could be drawn. Kruth knew from experience that the merest gesture from a sorcerer could cause death, no matter how ancient or decrepit the hand.

Kruth despised magic, except for certain bedroom elixirs.

There were also many rumors about the Shadow Walker's armor. Dense plates as dark as a devil's backside, the color of a moonless sky, yet almost weightless. Some said it allowed the wearer to remain unseen by the naked eye. A phantom moving without notice, a deadly shadow killing without obstacle. Kruth could see how such armor could benefit a thief. Or assassin.

Still more said the armor rendered the wearer invulnerable. It was tailored from the skin of a dragon. The scales could deflect any weapon. The strongest of swords shattered on impact. Arrows were like the merest of gnats. You could walk through fire and not feel the flames.

Kruth pondered all the rumors and myths. What one could do with such armor?

Even if the armor proved to be a myth, the mission would no doubt prove profitable. And if the armor did exist?

The world, like a whore in the King's personal harem, would be at your feet.

Thirty men, the elite of Tyrannis personal guard, had accompanied him. None were left. Just as well, mused Kruth. Less to kill on the journey home. Still, he would not have minded another set of eyes and swords protecting his back.

The King's seer, a drug-addled dolt named Sarzer, saw in a vision (or so he said) dangers that would befall the journey.

"Keep close sword and spear, and closer fear, when the tree people near," he said between rib-rattling coughs.

True enough, a forest bordered the Eastern lands, the trees as plentiful as lies in a harlot's mouth. The sky was a canopy of vines and leaves. The archers were at the ready, bows held high, aiming for any enemy from above. It was only when a tree uprooted itself and gave chase that the seer's vision proved true.

Tree people indeed.

Arrows swarmed like hornets to no effect. Swords hacked off branches while branches pierced men like fruit. Tyrannis' guards flew though the air like fallen leaves.

Two-thirds of the men were dead or scattered before Kruth lit a torch.

The tree people made for good kindling. The few surviving guardsmen slept well and warm that night.

"Cross not unto the path of the unicorn's wrath," was another of Sarzer's visions.

Kruth had never seen a unicorn but had heard tales of their beauty, their unrivaled majesty. They were said to be as white as a Storm giant's beard in winter and their horn believed to contain magical properties. Some said it possessed the secret of youth and vitality. Unicorns could outrun an arrow and never had one been saddled or ridden. They were rare creatures, only captured in stories. Kruth never expected to see one other than in tapestries or molded in clay.

When the unicorn finally appeared, it was neither beautiful nor majestic. Kruth could see why it was said they could not hold a rider. It burst forth from a growth of trees (the non-chasing kind) a mass of muscled destruction. Kruth, truth be told, was disappointed. The unicorn was an unthinking brute, common as found in any tavern or sprawled drunk in the gutter, and about as graceful. This one was four-footed, hide an elephant-gray, and just as thick. It reminded Kruth of the bulls of his youth. Stupid animals but so large they commanded respect, lest a misplaced hoof break one's foot. Or rib. True, the beast did have a horn, two in fact, one longer, one shorter, and the horns did contain the secret of youth.

The three men it gored never aged a single day again.

Three men wore holes in their guts and another five trampled by heavy hoof, before the beast tasted deep of Kruth's sword. The blow, struck right behind the unicorn's left knee, caused the animal to buckle. It was short work after that, the throat being an easy target. Kruth's right hand was wet with unicorn's blood.

After it was butchered and braised, the beast tasted as good as it looked. Rat served raw had more flavor. Still fresh meat was fresh meat.

Any survivors had scattered. At daybreak, Kruth alone set out again with the horns as trophies.

It was another three days before he cleared the forest. In the clearing stood a structure unlike any Kruth had seen before. He had heard tales of floating cities and temples sunk beneath green seas. He had seen with his own eyes underground societies populated by the dead and those who should have been. Nothing had prepared him for this. The majestic structure appeared to be a triangle on all sides. The geometry defied logic. Surely, this was wrought by sorcery or unknown alchemy, Kruth thought.

At its base, Kruth saw the temple was composed of stone. Touch confirmed that. Huge blocks moved either by slaves, beast or magic; Kruth didn't know, still he was amazed. He stared at its top, nearly lost in the clouds. He traveled the length of each side; no entrance was to be found. At least, not at a walker's level. Further up, Kruth spied a spot of blackness. It was too perfect in a shape to be a mere shadow; nothing was high enough to cast shade on the structure. Kruth hoped it was a door; it was worth investigating at the very least.

To most this would have marked the journey's end. But not to one who had traveled and trained with Aranos of the Spiders Guild, worshipper of Oxyopes, the Spider God. Kruth had spent months of his youth as a traveling companion to the noble paladin Aranos on many adventures. True, he might not be able to scurry up the sides of the monument as fast as the four-armed Aranos or as graceful, but his one-time companion would have been proud of him. Having a length of rope spun from Spiders Guild web didn't hurt. It was well nigh unbreakable and could support twice a unicorn's weight.

Securing the rope, Kruth began the long climb. Fingers dug into seams as big as a crow's eye. Muscles strained and screamed. The pain was great. Kruth was use to pain. It was his life. It was the way of a warrior. Eventually, the pain passed. It was then an exercise of patience and strength.

The Valley of Shadows was well named; the sun didn't become a factor until he was over half way up the structure. It wasn't the heat, but Kruth's own sweat that made every handhold treacherous. If his grip betrayed him, death waited below.

The journey continued. Muscle against stone, muscle against muscle until Kruth made his way to the entrance, inch by agonizing inch. And it was an entrance; neither door nor wall barred the path. The opening stood as tall as five grown men and Kruth remembered the tale of the Shadow Walker standing shoulder to shoulder with giants. A shudder passed through him, worth mentioning only because the feeling was a stranger to him.

Beyond the entrance, darkness welcomed. Thirty steps forward, sunshine slowly retreating with every step, was a hole, a pit. The air smelled sour-sweet, like meat left too long in the sun. Staring down the hole, Kruth could make out the flicker of what he hoped were torches.

Curses that he didn't have the eyesight of a hawk or an owl, or a spell to replicate either predator's vision.

Kruth had not survived this long by strength and swordplay alone. He knew he was tired and needed rest; the climb had drained him. The Shadow Walker would have to wait. He thought of his current situation; escape was seemingly impossible. Only one man would walk out of this temple alive.

If he survived, Kruth would be demanding all of Tyrannis' daughters as his wives and more importantly a King's dowry for each.

After a few hours of rest, he once again set forth. He unwound the web rope and began the slow climb down. Fortunately, going down was less strenuous than the climb up had been.

When his feet met the ground, he surveyed what lay before him.

A great hall was buried in the belly of the temple, ill lit save for a half dozen torches. They illuminated an altar-throne made of bone. Human or otherwise, Kruth could not tell. The throne sparkled, catching the torches' light. Jewels the size of a man's fist decorated the throne. And on the throne, sat a collection of cloth. The collection of cloth moved, sniffed the air, like a hound turned loose on the hunt. The robes concealed an old man, Kruth judged by the slowness of his movement, every gesture a contest with internal pain. The Shadow Walker was well named, for his wrinkled skin was dark as pitch.

Kruth had fought his way out of the Pain Pits where everyday was a battle for survival. He had survived the tree people, crushed snakes that could swallow men with his bare hands, and killed the vampire man-bat of the Skaarlands, slitting the beast's throat, leaving it to choke on stolen blood. That deed had been done left-handed too.

The old man didn't stand a chance.

"I see you. Step out of the shadows. This is my home. There is no place to hide. Come out, little morsel, and introduce yourself."

"I am Kruth, ambassador to the God-King Tyrannis. At his request, I come to deliver his message of peace."

The old man slowly moved off the throne.

Kruth could see the wizened figure bore resemblance to the other Easterners he'd seen, the same irregular eyes, but none with skin this dark.

The old man spoke.

"Spare me your message. I'm assuming it's the same message as those who came before. I took you for a warrior, a soldier at the very least. Not an echo, not an errand boy."

Gripping his sword hilt, Kruth circled the stooped bundle of rags.

"Old man, I am Kruth. I am neither echo nor errand boy. I offer peace but will take your head in its place. I'm here for your life, your treasure, and your fabled armor. Prepare to taste cold Skarvanian steel and be damned. I am your death."

The old man hissed, "I am called Apep, as my father and my father's father was called. Perhaps, you have heard also of my legendary fighting prowess just as you have heard of my fabled armor, black as sin, black as devil's grin. Consider this a gift, morsel, before we begin the dance I have danced so many times before. This is the gift I bequeath to you, Kruth, warrior born. The truth I give before you welcome death's crushing embrace."

"I am not the greatest of my kind, merely the last. We were ancient when you were learning to crawl. And the armor... that is a lie too." Taking a breath. Apep whispered, "A lie. No, not a lie. The armor does exist but it is not armor."

"Spare me your riddles," Kruth growled.

"A mystery is it not, my friend. Armor that is not armor. Fear not, all shall be revealed. My gift to you." He paused. "It is dragon skin, the skin of a dragon. My skin."

As the old man Apep smiled, teeth like daggers, his muscles contorted, spasmed as his skin expanded, the cloth ripped away, great wings unfurled like the coming of night, smoke curled from dragon nostrils.

Kruth assumed a fighter's stance, sword arm high. Again a cold shudder as he remembered the God King's seer's third and final vision.

"Beware if you dare the dragon skin wear."

THE GUESTS

Beneath an October moon, a mother and son prepare themselves for their nocturnal visitors. They scoop orange guts and carve eyes where there are none, place a candle to serve as substitute brain. Bowls are filled with chocolate ears and peanut-butter eyes, licorice worms and Gummi rats. The son samples a candy tarantula, his teeth stained an unnatural red. Outside stationary skeletons stand sentry while cheesecloth spirits dance in strobe light. All is ready. Almost.

"Can I put on my costume on now?" asks the son, already half dressed.

The mother nods her approval. The son dons the rest of his costume and adjusts his mask.

"How's it look?"

"Almost human," the mother grins, an army of needles not quite concealed behind her smile.

MONSTER BURGER

Jerome rubbed his eyes and stared at the atrocity across the street. It was a nightmare of angles, the by-product of deranged architectural design. His eyes hurt just looking at the garish colors and weird geometry.

The hard-hatted workers, probably illegals judging by their accents, a strange combination of grunts, growls and the occasion expletive, had worked quickly and efficiently, like dwarfs high on meth, in order to complete the job. The building opened its doors for business a month ago in the lot once occupied by Dogs and Suds, a local eatery equally famous for their chili-dogs and the indigestion they produced. Lunchtime at D n' S (as it was known by the locals) was like facing a firing squad at Fort Fart.

The former owner Danny Markland had sold the business and fled to the warmer climes of Florida. Bastard. Didn't even say anything to Jerome about the sale. Maybe the skin cancer fairy would pay Danny a visit or he would be stomped to death by a stampede of geriatric beach walkers. He pictured a tanned Danny, belly eclipsing his feet, watching bikini-clad bimbos saunter while sucking down Margaritas like an overweight mosquito.

Jerome felt the dull throb of a headache working behind his eyes. He squinted at the gothic arches, man-made monstrosities of welded metal. Damn ugly things. Steel spider webs complete with giant fiberglass arachnids. They were better suited for a cemetery or decorating a European castle beneath black and white skies than a restaurant. Ugly as it was, it also worked. The gimmick was a guaranteed moneymaker. Monster Burger was busier than the St. Michaels Church Festival beer stand at last call. The drive-thru did brisk business as well. Always bumper to bumper during the lunchtime rush. Jerome would have guessed the novelty of ordering through a grinning skull (it glowed in the dark at night, too) would have worn off by now. No such luck. That worried him; he was losing customers and money. He wasn't sure how the Fish Shack, the business his father and grandfather before him had built, was going to survive.

The real pisser was it could have been Jerome on the beach, not Danny. He could've been soaking up the sun, suds and surf. The Monster Burger owner, Mister Woebegon, offered to buy him out. Although it was the family business, Jerome didn't have any family to pass the Fish Shack on to. His sister, Tonya, had her own business to occupy her time. He wasn't getting any younger either. He had hoped Woebegon would up his offer, something to add to the old retirement fund. Better a chance of pigs learning to pilot planes before that would happen now.

The town of Chagrin Falls didn't have much in the way of restaurants. Truth be told, Chagrin Falls didn't have much of anything. It was a town that when passing through, if you dared blink, you'd miss the two local bars, the police station and local theatre (with a single screen and dollar hot dogs), or Ernie Rednose, the town drunk, permanently affixed to a bench on Main Street. Monster Burger was the first fast-food restaurant chain in Chagrin Falls. Jerome, along with the town council and other citizens, was glad when he first heard the news. It was a sign of progress, the last since the library added computers and rolled out the electronic welcome mat of Internet porn to its patrons. He was just pissed Monster Burger set up shop so close to him.

Damn that Danny Markland. Maybe he would be mistaken for a baby whale and be accidentally harpooned.

Jerome met with Mr. Wobegon as soon as he learned about the deal that led to Danny's departure, offering Wobegon and his work crew free food as a gesture of good will. Curiously, the workers always seemed to brown bag their lunches. Damn sure weren't giving the Fish Shack any business. He thought it would serve as an opportunity to size up Wobegon, see the nature of the beast, so to speak. He didn't look forward to it. His previous impression was similar to stepping in dog shit. Five minutes with Wobegon left you with a smell you couldn't quite shake.

At just under five feet tall, Mr. Wobegon looked like he was part man, part warthog and all ugly. Jerome guessed his mother carried him by his lower jaw as a child, much like one would hold a bowling ball. To say his jaw stuck out would be like saying a skunk had stink. Irregularly shaped teeth hid behind a lower lip better suited to an ape. He was just missing the humpback that would have made him the ideal spokesman for Monster Burger. He made dead possums look positively cuddly.

"So good to see you again, Mr. Jerome. Always a delight. As you can see, we're not open for business yet. But soon. Very soon. Chomping at the bit, or as we like to say, chomping at the burger. Yes. To what do I owe the pleasure?"

Jerome felt like he had just sipped the finest tea in the world only to discover the label read elephant urine. Jerome wasn't sure what Wobegon was selling but he sure as hell wasn't buying. He spoke his piece, welcoming him to the neighborhood, and the bit about the free food.

Wobegon, all manners and charm and snaggled toothed, said, "I don't like fish. Nasty creatures. All fins and scales. No meat. You keep them. I never eat fish. "

And that was that.

Still, he had to give the devil his due; Monster Burger made a damn good burger. He ate there the opening week, wanted to check out the competition. Besides, they had a buy one Monster Burger, get one Monster Burger free special running. Jerome couldn't resist a good deal. From their Chocolate Ooze shakes (50 cents more for extra ooze) to their French-fried Monster fingers to their Heart Stopper burger, three patties of lean ground beef topped with your choice of toppings, their menu had more selections than Stumpy Bill's Blade-a-Rama had knives.

The interior looked more like a combination spook house/haunted laboratory than a restaurant. The cooks sported the latest in mad scientist fashion and customized butcher aprons, complete with blood-splattered Monster Burger logos. Mr. Wobegon, all smiles, directed traffic. The cashier, dressed like a witch, placed orders on a tombstone-shaped register.

Jerome recognized the witch. Melissa had worked at the Fish Shack up until two weeks ago. Damn. Not only stealing his customers but his employees too. Melissa was a damn good worker, as pretty as she was reliable. At only 16, she had a maturity beyond her years and a cheerleader's enthusiasm. She was also Spanish Club President and a member of the Honor Society.

With a wink and a smile to let her know there were no hard feelings, Jerome gave Melissa his order.

"Would you like to Monster size that?"

The Fish Shack was definitely in trouble.

And as things turned out, so was the town. Chagrin Falls was relatively crime-free. There was the occasional Klan rally populated mostly by the curious and the illiterate, the runaway cow to catch, some teenage vandalism and some people-old-enough-to-know-better vandalism. There was the dogcatcher who went on a killing spree a few years ago but every town had at least one kook who inspired stories to scare children. The cops busied themselves arresting drunks and investigating library smut complaints.

Domestic disturbance calls were on the upswing. The crime report in *The Chagrin Falls Gazette* was now a whole page where it once occupied a paragraph. Blackmail, drug use and acts of violence became as commonplace as ants at a picnic. And that was just on the playground.

It was a subtle change. Where once people left their doors unlocked, now Biddle's Hardware did brisk business selling security lights, locks and Forget-The Dog-Beware-Of-Owner signs. People stayed in more. Dogs barked less. The Fish Shack continued to lose business. The changes took their toll on everyone. Even Monster Burger. Jerome noticed they had added a new menu item, the Sea Creature sandwich, priced a whole 50 cents cheaper than the Fish Shack special, not including fries. Not that it could ever compete with the flavor of Jerome's catfish recipe, filets marinated in beer and liberal doses of Tabasco, then rolled in a combination of black pepper, cayenne pepper, bread crumbs, flour and cornmeal. But people weren't lining up for the Sea Creature or the Fish Shack special like they use too.

It was like someone had placed a black garbage bag over the town and was beginning to twist.

*   *   *

Jerome was helping Charley, his newest employee, change the Fish Shack sign.

"Try to undercut me, will they," Jerome thought. "We'll see about that."

Jerome handed a number 9 in the form of a fish to Charley.

"Why didn't you apply to Monster Burger?"

Charley, wiping the sun from his eyes, grimaced. "I did. They turned me down. They wanted me to work Sundays. Couldn't. Church."

Jerome nodded and handed Charley another 9.

*   *   *

It was a rainy day. Gray clouds flopped across the sky like a stringer of trout. Jerome arrived at the Fish Shack early and noticed a solitary figure sitting in the Monster Burger parking lot. He stepped out of his truck and saw the slouching figure was Melissa, his former employee. Her yellow poncho was soaked. She looked like a mutated banana.

She had been crying, although it was tough to distinguish tears from the raindrops streaking her face. He offered his hand and helped her inside.

Handing her a towel, Jerome asked what was wrong.

"School okay?"

"Affirmative."

"Family good?"

"Never better."

"Boyfriend trouble?"

"Negative."

"You didn't fall in love with a midget sword swallower and have plans joining the circus as his assistant?" Silence. "Well…"

"Ick. What are you, some perv?"

"Just a concerned perv. Come on. What's wrong?"

Melissa opened up.

"I dunno. It's just … well, yesterday Mr. Wobegon asked me to come in early today. No big deal, right? But it's Mom's birthday, and I told him so. He questioned my loyalty to the store, if I would ever be grown up enough, mature enough, to handle adult responsibilities, after all there will always be another birthday and on and on. By the time he was finished, I felt too embarrassed and ashamed not to show up to work today."

"Christ, I'm only 16 and it's just a job punching buttons, and I feel like I'm letting Mr. Wobegon down by not showing up. I don't even like the guy that much. He's creepy, always talking to himself. And the way he watches us, not just me, but the other employees and even customers. It's like he thinks were gonna steal something. It's like watching a nature documentary. He's one of those bugs you don't see until it's gobbling up another bug."

Jerome passed her a cup of steaming coffee.

"Welcome to the real world, Mel. Go home, help your mom blow out her candles. There's still a job waiting for you at the Fish Shack. If you want it. And a raise too."

"You can't mean that. Your business has been way down. You can't…"

Jerome cut her off. "We always take care off our own. Remember that."

Jerome remembered when Melissa's father took off on her mom, no note, no phone calls, no child support. The town helped raise that girl. Not too bad a job at that.

"Go home. Grey skies today but weatherman Jerome predicts sunny days ahead," he said with a wink. "You can start back Monday and when school starts back up, we'll work out a schedule."

After another day of less than stellar sales, Jerome went home and phoned his older sister.

While Jerome Sr. might have had a green thumb when it came to agriculture, that skin pigment was not inherited by his offspring. As a traditional farmer, Tonya could only grow closer and closer to bankruptcy. But as an aquaculture pioneer, she was raking in the greenbacks as easy as shucking corn. Tonya raised catfish and perch and even goldfish. Ten thousand of them in a walled-off section of what used to be the family farm. The barn now housed conveyer belts and walls of aquariums. Nine giant plastic tanks held schools of fish. Fins everywhere. The scaly students were destined for stocking local ponds or deep fryers and frying pans.

"Sure it was a crazy idea, but so was selling bottled water or growing worms for Vend-A-Bait machines. I wish I'd hatched those ideas first, too," Tonya was fond of saying. "But Mama, God rest her britches, always said you should do what you love, and I've always loved catfish. Eating or catching. Doesn't matter."

It was true, aside from being blood-related, Tonya and Jerome were fishing buddies since they were half the size of a cane pole. They learned how to tie knots, bait hooks and the fine art of noodling together.

Noodling, or "hand grabbing" as the sport is also known, involved catching catfish with your hands. There was a danger factor. You ran the risk of snakes, muskrats and drowning. Tonya's ruined right hand was testimony to that. She used part of the insurance payout as seed money for the fish farm.

Success didn't come easy. The first batch floated; every single fish dead. But the second grew to sandwich size and the business was born.

Jerome was proud of his sister's success. Although they didn't see each other often (Tonya was frequently on the road preaching the profits of the fish business), Jerome still respected his sister's opinion. And it was her farm-raised filets the Fish Shack served.

She answered on her cell phone, a little north of Nashville, heading towards a fish hatchery.

Jerome told her of his problems with Monster Burger eating up his customers and the melancholy that had permeated the town thick as chicken gravy.

Tonya had heard the rumors and wondered why Jerome's last fish order was so low. She reminded him of the tough times their dad went through, the tough times she went through. Sometimes sacrifices had to be made. Jerome rubbed his head, thinking of his sister's flipper for a hand. He said he loved her and hung up, decisions dancing in his head like canaries on fire.

The rain continued. It was like the heavens had loaded up at the celestial bar on quarter beer night and were pissing away their sorrows. Even cats were learning to dog paddle. The rain came down like paratroopers, crazy for war.

Jerome was feeling a little crazy himself. With nothing on the tube—storms had screwed up the cable—Jerome went for a drive.

He passed the Sav-A-Lot, Bauer's Ford dealership and the local doughnut shop. Too bad it was closed. He could really go for a pair of bear claws. He continued driving, making a stop here and there, filling the tank, and ended up in the southern end of town, out near the fairgrounds.

He veered off US 52 and took the gravel road, over the railroad tracks where some of the older locals still swore they heard the Ghost Train and its skeletal engineer in the wee hours of the night. Jerome didn't put much stock in Ghost Train stories. After a night of fishing and drinking, Jerome's old man swore he had just narrowly missed being splattered by the spectral train.

"Damn thing flew off the tracks and aimed right for me, the bony conductor laughing like mad. I still hear his teeth rattle in my nightmares sometimes."

He said he survived by diving down a hill and rolling into the bushes, thorns be damned. Busted up his chin, required seven stitches and would proudly show you the scar. Jerome later heard from Tonya who heard the truth from Mom. Part of the story was true. Dad was filled to the gills, tripped and caught the business end of a hoe in the face. Jerome remembered once getting his dad a brand new hoe for his birthday and the look on his face seemed to validate Tonya's version of the story.

Jerome glanced at his watch. An hour and 15 minutes until midnight.

The gravel road turned into mud. He continued driving, watching the lightning bugs play hide and seek beneath the canopy of leaves. Jerome thought about the woods. He'd been coming here since he was a kid, riding his bike at night. Unless, you had experienced it, you really had no idea how dark the woods could be, how alive they seemed even with the lights off. It spooked him a little. Jerome could hear the river directly in front of him. He turned off the ignition.

No one seemed to be doing any night fishing tonight. Occasionally, you'd see a lantern or the bright end of a cigarette. The rain must have kept everyone away. Further downstream was a campground and you could usually hear the raucous laughter of canoers, setting up camp and knocking down cold ones. Tonight the woods were silent, save for the river and the rain.

The locals called this area the Point, where the east and west forks of the Whitewater River crossed. The water was anything but white tonight. Days of rain and runoff had turned the rapids the color of chocolate milk. Beneath the moon, it looked black, a watery abyss. There had always been stories about the Point as a place where wishes came true. The real truth was it served better as a condom graveyard than a wishing well.

"Might as well get it over with," he said to one in particular.

He pulled off the truck's tarp. Mr. Wobegon was in the back.

One of his stops on the way to the Point was Monster Burger. Seemed that Wobegon had never gotten around to changing the locks. The key Danny gave Jerome when he first opened Dog and Suds worked. Quiet as a deer hunter stalking a buck, he let himself inside.

Wobegon was in his office, talking to himself. The trouble with talking to yourself was you never who was listening. Jerome suffered the same problem. The office was about as big as a closet. Jerome, not wanting to scare the Monster Burger owner, lightly tapped on the door.

"Mister Jerome. We are closed. Come back in a few hours for breakfast. Our Alien omelet is to die for."

Jerome stood his ground.

"I knew it was only a matter of time. You see, Monster Burger is a very large organization, a very old organization. Our pockets run very deep. Indeed we are ingrained into this country's very fabric. You've probably seen the ads. Your country's founding fathers or at least their facsimiles, eating our famous burgers. Washington, Lincoln, Elvis supping on our delicious cuisine. We have franchises in thirty-five states, even Alaska, and are always growing."

Wobegon rolled up his sleeves and continued.

"Our ways have changed. We no longer operate under the confines of the night. The sun shines on us now. We accepted consumerism as the new religion. Your townspeople pay homage in our church everyday, just like they do all over the world. My heart smiles just thinking about it. You could have had a place in our organization. Granted, not a high position but even Hell needs its garbage collectors, Heaven its janitors. But you turned us down. Not acceptable."

Jerome listened to everything Wobegon said. He was right. Jerome had spent some time in college, taken accounting, marketing, economics and finance classes, before assuming the reins of the Fish Shack. He knew all about the Monster Burger business plan. Their success couldn't be denied. Besides, the food was good.

Jerome had also had some physics classes. He calculated five pounds of frozen Monster Burgers patties with just the right of amount of momentum would pack one hell of a wallop. He nailed Wobegon right between the eyes, dropping him faster than the Prom Queen's panties after the final dance.

The first blow had only stunned Wobegon. Jerome reckoned it was blows seven or eight that finally sent him off to fast food heaven. Even as a kid, Jerome hated to see anything suffer.

Looking out across the river, Jerome's remembered his dad saying, "Respect the river and it will respect you."

The river was shallow here but several yards out it dropped off noticeably. It was along this ledge where Tonya had lost her fingers. They had been warned about the area. Everyone in town knew the stories, just like everyone knew about the Ghost Train. They were just stories. Jerome thought the same thing until he watched the thing that had chewed his sister's fingers off swim away. Wasn't like any muskrat or catfish he'd ever seen. Muskrats didn't have fins and catfish didn't have legs and neither animal grew to that size, had teeth that big or numerous.

Jerome called it Whiskers. He had never seen the creature again. Just the same he knew it was out there. It was older than the town. That he did believe.

He had feelings of déjà vu, remembering being here with Melissa's father, shortly after his drug habit caused him to assault both wife and daughter, putting Mel in the hospital. Another time with Stuart Anderson who liked little children a bit too much. With others. Nameless. Countless. The town took care of its own.

He gently pushed Wobegon into the water. The current caught the body. It swiftly went under. Jerome had weighted the body down with frozen patties. Catfish were bottom feeders after all.

Jerome knelt and placed his hands in the water, whispered, "And your soul to keep." He dried his hands on his shirt and returned to the truck.

*   *   *

As he drove in to open the Fish Shack the following day, a fire engine blocked the road. Monster Burger was charbroiled, the spiders still smoking.

Ernie "Rednose" Miller, full-time drunk and part-time volunteer fireman gave Jerome the details.

Evidently, sometime around three 3 a.m., Monster Burger went up in flames. Pretty quick considering how wet the structure was with all the rain. The restaurant appeared to be empty. Ernie guessed electrical fire.

With the Fish Shack in Melissa's capable hands, Jerome returned to the Point a few days later, a picnic lunch and a *Chagrin Falls Gazette* under his arm. The fire captured the front page. Mr. Wobegon had disappeared according to the article. Arson was being considered. The insurance company bought that hook, line and sinker. All requests for comments from Monster Burger's corporate office had been met with a firm "no comment."

Jerome could barely make out footprints. It looked like a print a duck would make, if the duck wore a size 16, extra-wide in the flipper. He smiled. Wobegon said he didn't eat fish. Pity, the opposite wasn't true.

Weeks passed. Mr. Wobegon never surfaced. Jerome received a postcard from Danny. A picture of perfect female asses in thongs with the caption "Just Bumming Around." Once the excitement of the fire died down, boredom settled over the town like a low-lying fog. The crime report in the paper shrunk in size. The big news was a new restaurant would be opening. Setting up shop in one of the empty spaces along main street, the Pork Barrel. That was fine with Jerome. He loved BBQ.

PICNIC IN THE WOODS

They watched and waited. Given enough time, their patience would pay off. Past experience had proven all it took was time and, of that precious commodity, they had plenty. Their moment would arrive. No doubt about it. It was only a question of when. And so they waited, hidden from view, watching the river, the current, crest, whirl and fall, oblivious to passing seconds and the world.

This was Richard's first canoeing experience, one he was not enjoying. Part of the problem being he was still hung over from the night before. An assortment of shots, whiskey and rum with tequila as the exclamation point. Daggers to the skull, a recipe for disaster. His head felt like the snare drum for a Norwegian death metal band. The other, bigger problem was his fellow canoer Keith. Bad enough he worked with the dick, sharing cubicle space so small you could sublet to a family of Mexicans; he didn't relish sharing his weekends with this asshole too. But Evelyn, Richard's fiancée, and Keith's wife Marcy were friends from college, spirit squad cheer sisters at that, and Richard had been cajoled (with the promise of still undelivered blow jobs) into what was fast becoming the worst camping experience of his life.

"You gotta watch this river. It's crafty as a cable TV televangelist," Keith said knowingly. "The current will grab you faster than a convulsing whore giving a handjob. You hear me, Dick? I'd hate to see you wet your shorts."

"I hear you," muttered Richard, adjusting his crotch through his blue jean cutoffs. *I got your Dick right here,* he thought to himself.

Suddenly, the canoers heard a whistling in the air then BANG. Followed by BANG, BANG, BANG.

Marcy was screaming like she was giving birth to sextuplets. Keith stood up, making himself the perfect target and properly nose-dived into the water, just avoiding the speeding projectile.

Richard shouted over the noise, "It's only fireworks. Probably some goddamn kids shooting off bottle rockets."

After regaining his footing in the water, Keith stormed, "Jesus Christ on a crutch! Fuckers nearly shot me in the head! I'm gonna kill the little bastards! I'm gonna…" Keith was cut short by a tearful Marcy.

"You aren't going to do anything but get us the hell out of here. This was your stupid idea, and I'm sick of it. Sick of the bugs, the fucking weather, the water and most of all, sick of you. First you forget to pack my meds, then you schedule this trip on my mother's motherfucking birthday! And the King Kong kicker? You keep staring at Evelyn's muffin-sized tits the whole time we're out here! Don't think I haven't noticed. Fuckin' perv."

Evelyn, one arm covering her pastry-sized bosom, moved to console her friend. She also realized they were all still sitting ducks. "I think she's right. We should probably just go."

Richard, looking at the soaking Keith, now rendered speechless, thought that was the best news he had heard all day.

Beneath the trees, camouflaged by the woods, JJ was laughing through his tears. Pete was rolling on the ground. "Did you see that dude? He was like a flamin' flamingo with palsy."

"Yeah," answered JJ. "Another two inches and it would've been a head shot for sure. That was the best yet. I wish the chick in the tank top would've been the one in the water. Did you catch a gander at those tits? Bitching milking MILF'ers for sure, dude."

Using his blue bandanna to wipe the tears from his eyes, JJ asked if there was any beer left. Pete had stolen a few cans from his dad. Although it was warm, the beer went down smooth on a Sunday afternoon.

"Ready for the next round?"

"Absofuckinglutley, my friend. Here's to tourists and tits and fireworks made in Taiwan." The boys toasted each other and settled back into position, lighters and rockets at the ready. Watching and waiting, unaware they were also being watched.

After several minutes of inactivity, save bug swatting, JJ stood to take a leak. His piss just starting to stream when his head exploded in a fury of colors, painting the trees and staining the ground. Pete watched the cranial eruption as blood, brains, bone and bandanna flew everywhere. He stared in horror at his headless friend, like some surreal still life, when a hand more animal than man closed around his mouth, smothering his scream, and a yellow-fanged mouth descended, turning his neck to tatters.

Through blood stained teeth the creature grunted, "Uk. Brains best part. Now half only. Looked like bird scared of feather. Grimlick haw, haw, haw. Funny. Still eat all round."

The other monstrosity, after retrieving his throwing stone and slurping it clean, stuck a moss green claw through Pete's eyeball. The eye made a squishy noise, like pudding sucked through a straw.

"Raw good." The thing turned, lurching on unnaturally long legs, and sunk fingers like knives into JJ's still spurting stump.

The two trolls sat down for an impromptu picnic hidden beneath a canopy of leaves.

*   *   *

"What the hell was that?"

Clyde, pulling his paddle from the water, replied, "Dunno George. Kinda sounded like a burp."

"Jesus Christ. You didn't tell me there were bears in these woods."

"Shut up and row, George. And if you're not gonna row, make yourself useful and pass me another beer."

Doing as he was told, George pulled another can from their stringer of beers and the canoers floated gently down stream.

THE FISHERMAN

In the town of Winterhaven, fishing was a way of life. The first word out of an infant's mouth was more likely to be "bass" instead of "mama." Most children learned how to bait a hook before they were taught to tie their shoes. Men didn't discuss who would win the Super Bowl or the World Series; they didn't care. The bottom line was who would capture the Bass Master Classic and walk off with the coveted Angler of the Year award. In a town where TV fishing host Bill Dance was regarded as a saint and the local reverend spoke more of Jonah than Jesus in his sermons, Silas McGee was a fisherman among fishermen. And that's what caused Lester Wilkes to break more fishing poles than any five men in angler history.

Lester was a damn good fisherman. He could coax fish to bite when everyone else was already microwaving their fish sticks at home. He could seduce them with little more than spit and a paper clip. He was good.

Silas was a legend. He looked the part. He had more wrinkles than a fat lady had stretch marks and walked like the fat lady was riding piggyback. His face was so pale from walking hunched over one wondered if Silas ever saw the sky. The beard didn't help. It reached to his navel and was the color of a well-used toilet bowl.

Ancient as he was, he could be seen everyday with his brown bag of medicinals (as he liked to call the 40-ouncer), his rods and his can of bait, fishing to his heart's content. When the day was done, he left with the bottle empty and his stringer full.

Lester had an unhealthy distrust and dislike for Silas. Distrust because Lester distrusted anything older than he was, even though he was almost 27. Dislike because Silas was a better fisherman. Not that Lester would ever admit it. And there was another reason too.

As a little minnow, Lester had caught Silas with his dirty overalls around his ankles, masturbating with a fish. Lester was about 13 and was no stranger to masturbation. He milked the walleye himself. But to see this old hillbilly with a fish on his dick saying, "Bite it, bite it," with his eyes rolled back in his head was something else all together. When Silas realized he was being watched he turned to Lester and said, "Maybe you'd like to give your mouth a try, boy?" Lester lit out of there faster than a fart at a baked bean buffet.

As an adult, Lester had avoided Silas. Silas always smelled like he had just stepped in dog shit and had made it a point that both shoes got equal amounts. Hygiene was not a priority. Not that it was a high priority with Lester either. If some lady was kind enough, dumb enough or drunk enough to spread her legs on Lester's face, he wouldn't wash for days instead letting the smell sit on his mustache so he could savor his conquest long after the battle was over.

Lester usually saw Silas' mug in the *Winterhaven's Gazette,* in the Catch of the Week feature. That damn goon face every week. He thought the paper should carry an advisory._*Warning: Extreme Ugliness may result in a loss of appetite.* Even if someone was reported missing or got caught desecrating one of the local graveyards, or someone found a ten-inch mushroom, Silas and his lunatic grin always took center stage.

There's no way in hell that increased sales, Lester swore.

Lester remembered last summer, when he had nailed a 15-pound large-mouth. Damned if he wasn't excited. He figured on being a lock for the Catch of the Week. No telling what kind of pussy he'd get being a celebrity. All smiles, he brought the fish to be weighed and the first thing the photographer said was, "That's the biggest fish I've seen all week except for the one Silas brought in this morning. Now that was a whopper!"

Lester shook his head, muttered something about "carp fucker" and smacked the photographer in the head with the bass. It was enough to make a man take up quilting.

Their paths had last crossed two weeks ago. Lester had taken the boat out, hoping to try a few holes in preparation for the upcoming walleye tournament. He had hoped to try a different kind of hole the night before without any luck. He took Mary Ellen out to eat. Slopped the hog but no pork was pulled.

He had been hung over as hell. The lake was anything but calm, causing Lester to heave his morning breakfast of Doritos, cold pizza and PBR into the water. Who should be there, but Silas with his $5.99 orange lifejacket and that rusted piece of shit he called a boat.

Lester steered well clear of the old man and started casting. To pass the time, he thought about all the pussy he didn't get last night. That started him thinking about all the beaver he hadn't tongued, fingered and banged over the years, which was a lot. Getting depressed, he imagined Silas was a modern-day Noah, but instead of gathering animals, he collected turds. Big turds, small turds, corn-filled, stinky feces of all imaginable geometric shapes. He imagined Silas's boat full of shit and still seeking more poop. Even when the boat began sinking, his quest for dung continued. With each turd, the boat sank a little more. Finally Silas noticed and panicked. There's too much shit.

Lester imagined himself sliding his boat up against Silas's, yanking his pants down and taking the crap of a lifetime, a gorilla shit, we're talking poop measured in pounds, right on to the steamy mound that was Silas's boat, sending that fish-sodomizing bastard into whatever watery Hell would have him.

Splashing woke Lester from his daydream. Maybe Silas's damn boat had sprung a leak. No such luck. Silas had caught another fish, about his seventh in the last hour. He put it on the stringer, took another hit from his bag, scratched his crotch and re-baited the hook.

Lester, using a big, fat night crawler imported from Texas, had caught nothing except for moss and the sniffles.

Super pissed, Lester yelled out, "Whatcha using for bait, Silas?"

Silas lowered the bag, sneered, then replied, "T'aint none of your damn business, boy."

With that, the fisherman reeled in his line, gunned the Mercury outboard and sputtered off across the lake, muttering as he went. After landing the remains of a tennis shoe, Lester returned to town to see if he could find out where the damned fish were biting. He was greeted with the best news of the day.

Apparently, Jerome Hickey had finally gotten tired of his fat wife and his equally obese kids and left them. No one had seen or heard from Jerome in the past ten days.

Lester thought Jerome was about as useful as a bleeding hemorrhoid. He was the type of guy who would smell his fingers after wiping his ass. Lester had knocked his front teeth out a few years ago in a heated argument over which color of Roostertail, white or yellow, was more effective for trout. Lester had screwed Jerome's wife Martha, too. Sweat meat.

Meat was the word for Martha, all 240 pounds of her. For a cow, she sure did have a tight pussy. She had a little Hitler Mustache on her snatch. Lester always gave her a Sieg Heil salute when she dropped her drawers. And could she suck peter? With such force, it would make your asshole cringe. Lester planned to go over and comfort her when he had time.

Jerome had been one of the odds on favorite to win the walleye tournament and the $500 that went along with it. With him out of the picture, Lester was thinking of ways to spend the prize money. Maybe treat Martha to a meal at Big Don's Barbecue—We pork it and you fork it.

Days passed. There was still no sign of Jerome. With the tournament a few days away, Lester was talking to P.J., his best friend and beer-drinking buddy. The first time they had met in grade school, P.J. was charging people a dollar to smell his finger. There was quite a line. P.J. said he had fingered Rosie Lee Marshall, every male fifth grader's jerk off fantasy, at last night's school carnival and had yet to wash his hand. Lester was skeptical but stink was still stink. Opportunities like this didn't arrive every day. Sure enough, there was a distinctive odor. A few months later in detention hall, P.J. revealed that he had stuck his finger in a can of tuna before arriving at school. He had cleared almost 30 bucks.

They were at P.J.'s combo junkyard and used car lot, plenty drunk, and talking about the usual: fishing, fucking and fighting, when Lester mentioned his meeting on the lake with Silas.

"Don't surprise me none. He's a sneaky bastard," said P.J.

"I don't know what he was casting, but it was working."

"Yeah, for a man who looks as if he's older than Methuselah, he sure as hell has brought in some biggun's. Surprised he ain't had a stroke yet, bringing some of them in," replied Lester.

"That Silas, he's a living breakfast. Flakes, fruits and nuts all in one bowl," snickered P.J.

At that, both men broke out laughing. Wiping tears from his eyes, P.J. said, "Yeah, I sure as hell wish I knew what the old geezer was using for bait."

"So do I," agreed Lester, his face as contorted as a question mark.

Later that evening, after being rejected by Martha, the blond clerk at the gas station, two teenagers walking home (damn dykes) and after downing a few more beers and flexing the five knuckle shuffle while watching a rerun of *Baywatch*, Lester had an idea.

Under the camouflage of night, Lester drove his pick-up to Silas' shack in the woods. Not taking any chances, he parked out of sight and staggered the rest of the way, stopping to answer nature's call once as he went.

Silas wasn't poor, but you couldn't tell that by his living conditions. His home was a log cabin that looked more like a log pile. In his yard were the remains of five cars. It was like a demolition derby and all the cars had come there to die. An outhouse stood near the shack. Judging from the grunts coming from within, the king was on his throne, thought Lester. With that bit of information, drunk on courage and cheap beer, he headed for the shack. The door already opened, he entered.

Inside he saw a couch that had seen better days, the remains of a chair that had seen much better days and a broken television with an axe firmly embedded in the screen that would never see the light of day again. Trophies of fish decorated the walls. Bass, catfish, walleye, bluegill, the place looked like a mounted aquarium. It smelled of beer, fish and urine. It was like a garbage can with windows and the windows were closed. Damn, it stank.

He moved into the kitchen. More fish decorated the walls. On the stove were some fresh bluegill, fried in cracker crumbs and another type of meat. His stomach growling, Lester sampled it. The fish was delicious and the meat mouthwatering. Kind of like squirrel but less gamey. Was that a fucking hair? It was. More than one. Didn't affect the taste, Lester thought as he swallowed.

Lester opened the refrigerator and found it empty, except for what looked like potato salad gone mutant, a jar of pickles and some baloney. He wondered what Silas did with all of his catch. Surely, it had to be here somewhere. He moved towards the window and tripped. He looked down and saw a handle. The entrance to the cellar.

Descending the narrow staircase, Lester looked around and saw poles, reels and tackle boxes galore. On a small worktable, among the knives, saws and hammers were lures by the hundreds, poppers, jigs, spoons, spinners, crankbaits and buzzbaits. Oddly enough, the lures looked as if they had not been used in quite some time. Rust covered the once glistening hooks. Pondering this, Lester saw an icebox in the corner of the cellar.

"So that's where the old man keeps his catch. He wouldn't mind if I borrowed some, would he. No sir," Lester said.

Lester opened the freezer. Among the packs of frozen fish and other meats was what remained of Jerome Hickey. His left arm was filleted to the bone. His right hand was missing three fingers.

Bile rising, Lester turned to puke. He looked into the worm-eaten, maggot-infested face of Wally "Whiskers" Malone who had disappeared months earlier. Scanning the room he saw bones and parts and pieces that caused him to gag. Hanging in a corner looked to be a skinned deer. But deer didn't wear Hanes underwear. Screaming "Jesus on a crutch!" Lester rushed upstairs and into Silas' murderous glare.

Instead of liquor or a fishing pole, Silas was holding an axe.

"So ya done gone and discovered my secret, did ya? Too bad, ya won't live to tell anyone. Usually, I like to use eight-pound Trilene monofilament to choke 'em. Sneak up all quiet like and snap. Just like crappie on a jig. But for a sneaky, gopher-cheeked peep thief like you, Betsy will do. Betsy, meet dead boy."

With the grace of a fly fisherman trying to catch a stubborn trout, Silas lifted the axe, lunged forward and fell down, gasping for breath.

Clutching his chest, Silas looked up into Lester's saucer wide eyes and whispered, "Shit. And I'm outta toilet paper too." Lester seized the opportunity. He kicked the fallen fisherman in the head once, twice, three times because it felt good.

Lester, regaining his composure, left as fast as his drunk-ass feet could carry him, staggering like a three-legged Daddy Longlegs back to his truck.

Lester reported his findings to the Sheriff Schlagsteiner who wrote him up on a public intoxication charge and put his ass in jail. The following morning, a hung over Lester explained what had happened. Skeptical at first, the sheriff agreed to check things out. An investigation was conducted. The coroner concluded that Silas really could've used a bath and that he died of heart failure. Four corpses, sixteen skeletons—including one horse skeleton—and an assortment of fingernails were found on Silas' property.

In wake of the grisly findings, Winterhaven's tourist population flourished. P.J. sold authentic fishhooks from the insane killer's very own tackle box made of human bone. At least he said they were authentic. Needless to say, he made a killing.

Widow Martha and her fatherless children became media darlings. In fact, Kirstie Alley was rumored to play Martha in Lifetime movie of the week. The walleye tournament was postponed and Silas made the front page for one last time. For once, Lester stole the spotlight. Everybody loved a hero. Although his sex life didn't improve much, Lester did receive a free Roland Martin signature series rod and reel courtesy of the local bait and tackle store, a free membership to B.A.S.S., ten spin-n-glow triple teasers and a set of *Baywatch* Season One DVDs.

Lester graced the cover of the Winterhaven Gazette several more times that year for winning four fishing tournaments and for breaking one county fishing record. A lot of people commented on the pictures, saying he looked fat. Lester shrugged it off, saying the camera always added at least 15 pounds. He didn't care. He was famous. In fact, his breaking the state record for striped bass even eclipsed the disappearance of little Amanda Southern and little Ricky Jameson for the headline in that week's paper.

THE ANGEL
AND THE ASS

The old jeep sounded like a prehistoric beast that had escaped extinction. It death-rattled its way down the dirt road. Sam drifted in and out of consciousness.

Oblivion was fast becoming his new best friend. Occasionally, he caught a glimpse of something, nothing familiar. A car up on blocks. An overgrown cemetery. A church with a sign in front saying, "Everybody smokes in Hell." He figured this must be the road to redneck Gehenna. Funny, he pictured it paved with crushed beer cans. Whatever his location, it was remote. No sign of streetlights, telephone wires or even clouds.

He'd always been headstrong, a chest-beater, a go-getter, an adrenaline main-liner. It served him equally well on the wrestling mat, on the football field and the war-torn streets of Bosnia. It's one thing to hear about a mass grave on the news, another to smell one. He'd learned first-hand about man's inhumanity to man. Years later, he still couldn't shake the stink. Once discharged, he vowed to make a difference.

He returned home to Detroit. His old man still lived there. Sam's father was tiptoeing into the early stages of dementia. Pops said he saw angels. They resembled girl scouts except for the feathers.

Sam went to college, studied criminology with a minor in theater. Got married, got divorced. He became a beat cop, wearing his shoes thin on the Motor City's hard streets.

He survived. His dad died. He moved up and moved on, joining the DEA. From the office to the underground to the deep fryer, he felt the sizzle.

The opportunity arose to "walk on the wild side" as his superiors put it. He grabbed it, saw it as a challenge, a chance to employ his education and experience. It was the role of a lifetime and he planned to ride it hard. His hair grew long and his beard woolly. From shoulder to elbow, he wore a sleeve of tattooed skulls. It was part of his new identity. His own mirror didn't recognize him.

He went undercover, six feet of dirt and then some. He banged heads and busted nuts, earning his rep as a bad, bad boy, working his way down south and up the drug chain. His current crew was a bunch of motorcycle misfits; a foul crowd called the Philistines. Their stock and trade was drugs, creating and distributing, with minors in murder.

The charade had worked. Sam was tight with sewage in human form named Evel Jenkins. Evel was the public face of the Philistines. Evel clocked in at about 180, was smart as whip and had a machine gun mouth. He was game show host material, could sell fire insurance to a pyromaniac.

Biker gangs had changed. Evolve or die. Evel was the link between the past and the future. A real estate salesman on his business card, it helped make inroads with the "haves," have money, have to spend it. He was a businessman who liked to ride. That's how he explained his unkempt biker companions. He organized the Toys for Tots run, the charity fish fries. He could out Kiwanis the Kiwanis when it came to community cheerleading. He was smoother than underage pussy and twice as dangerous.

His nickname was "Boyardee" because he could cook a batch that was pure paradise, sprinkled with brimstone. He was also a picky eater, preferring the unusual: opossums, eels, iguanas; he claimed to have sampled them all.

Sam hated the fucker. Not just because he was criminal scum, but because he was an ass. Dumb ass, stupid ass, jackass. He was a jock sniffer, couldn't stop talking smack about sports. Pro, college, pee wee. Evel was a diehard Lion's fan. Sam especially hated the Lions having lived in Detroit and had heard it all before. Evel talked for hours about last night's game, last week's game, last year's game. Sam had nothing against sports; he had enjoyed and excelled at them. But to just hear nonstop yak, the ceaseless drone—it was worse than Christmas with the relatives. He couldn't wait to put the fucker under.

The jeep stopped. The driver, a gent named Sasquatch due to his size, sanitary habits and missing-link looks, grabbed Sam by his shoulder length hair and yanked. Hands duct taped, Sam offered no resistance.

"Rise and shine, Tinkerbelle."

Sam groaned and stumbled to his feet. One eye was swollen shut courtesy of Sasquatch's ham hocks. He knew the place. Alligator Jack's bait shop before it burned down. The joint was still structurally sound although there hadn't been enough left of Jack to cremate.

Evel had said, "You haven't lived until you've had Kentucky Fried Jack. That's good jerky."

Sam didn't know if he'd been kidding.

The Philistines had converted the smoked house to a smoke house; it was a meth lab. The sign on the door still read, "Get hooked."

"Thanks for the valet service, Sassy," Sam said.

Sasquatch pulled Sam forward by his locks.

"Avon," Sam called and was pushed inside.

A single bulb lit the small room. The room reeked of paint thinner. It was a DIY chemistry set: Acetone, Drano, Iodine crystals, starter fluid, Hydrochloric Acid, Sulfuric Acid, Epsom Salts, Lithium batteries, Anhydrous Ammonia stored in propane tanks, Cold & Flu tablets. The place contained the makings of a real good time.

Evel sat on a 55-gallon steel drum. Standing between his legs was Sam's downfall. Del. She was an ass shaker, dream maker and heart breaker.

Del was a brunette, hair dark as Arctic midnight. She was an angel, fallen. Her curse to walk the Earth was mankind's blessing. Her curves had curves. Watching her walk was like watching a panther take down prey. Sam didn't have a chance.

They met at a 4th of July beach party. The crowd composed of a lot of people Sam didn't know. Evel made introductions as needed. Del was blowing up helium balloons for the kids. Her bikini looked like it was made from spider webs. Sam marveled that such tiny strands could contain such magnificent breasts. The voice was 100% Minnie Mouse due to too much helium intake.

"I'm Delilah, but everybody calls me Del," she squeaked. "My, my, my, you're a big one," she smiled staring at Sam's Bermudas. He was rock hard.

They shared a joint. Sam was already buzzed but his lips went nova when he took the first hit. Best grass he had ever tasted.

She had been born in New Orleans, lived there for years before moving. He could still hear the Creole in her voice. Del owned her own landscape company, both the legit business and the marijuana plants she harvested on the side. She was a woman who wasn't afraid to get her hands dirty.

A few beers and lines later, she said, "I've got a riddle for ya. What is sweeter than honey and stronger than a lion?"

Sam shrugged. He didn't enjoy riddles.

"I'll tell you later. If you're lucky," she said with a wink.

Later that night, deep between her thighs, Sam got the answer.

"My pussy."

Sam's cock thrust in agreement.

Del's orgasms were volcanic, her pussy leaked lava, and she shouted kaboom every time she came. She shouted it a lot.

They traveled to Orlando together. Evel wanted Sam to check out the scene, see if they could expand their operation, improve their lines of distribution. Evel knew about Sam's military background; he left his cop experience off the resume. Sam took Del along for company. They spent time on the beach, locked crotch to crotch. Sam had never seen water so clean and clear.

Later, he learned she was Evel's sister. By then, the barbs had been set.

Sam thought he could save the heroine and still lay the hammer on Evel. Del convinced him she wanted out; she'd seen too much, done too much. Evel had lost perspective, couldn't see the future. Thunderclouds were gathering. Sam offered her a door, a plea bargain, redemption. Turns out they were both liars.

Sasquatch dumped Sam to the floor, added a few kicks. Ash from the previous fire stuck to Sam's face.

"You fucked up, hippie. We took you in, called you brother, and you turn Judas. A fucking fed. There's no lower kind of snake. You know what we to do snakes around here? We cut off their stinking heads."

Evel pulled the six-inch lock blade from its hiding place and stepped closer.

Sam looked to Del. She looked away.

Sam struck, head-butting Evel in the face. Evel buckled. On the way down, Sam's knee pounded Evel's chin. The jolt traveled from jawbone to asshole and double backed. Sam, preparing to stomp the jackass' trachea, noticed movement to his left. Sasquatch.

Sam struck with a savate kick, "Coup de pied bas," French for "Bye-bye kneecap." The man-beast was down but not out. Before he could capitalize, Bang, Bang courtesy of a .44 Magnum. His shoulder burned. Thanks, Del. Then Sasquatch was on him. The Apocalypse arrived early.

Civilizations rose and fell. Mountains turned to dust. The universe kept on trucking and Sam finally woke up.

Little had changed. His head no longer hurt. The pain had changed from full tilt to a dull, gray throb. The odds were still against him.

Sasquatch, holding his injured knee, said, "You are one lucky son of a bitch. Lucky Del is such a piss-poor shot."

Evel was on the ground. A hole in his head.

"My brother was going to bring us all down. He sampled more than he sold. Careless. He let you in. You should have killed each other. Sibling killing sibling is a little too Shakespeare. He was my mad dog, my responsibility."

She wiped the snot from her nose.

Del stepped forward, holding Evel's knife.

"He was right about snakes, you know. We do cut off their heads."

She began to saw.

What a fucked up dream, Sam thought groggily. The edges slowly unblurred, things came into focus, and reality rolled out its welcome mat.

Del was standing next to Sasquatch. Evel was still dead. From Sam's turtle position, Del's hand grasped shadows. Her hand stroked the shadows. The shadows looked familiar. She held Sam's hair in her palm. He'd been scalped.

"Welcome back. You passed out from the shock. You've had a long day. I wanted you to be awake for this," she cooed.

"You're special. At first, I even wanted a souvenir. Such beautiful hair. The blackest I've ever seen. But that's sloppy and we know where sloppy gets you."

She nodded towards her dead brother.

"Don't want to end up like that. I want something more personal. Some cultures believe the eyes are the gateway to the soul. This is where it gets a little weird," she giggled.

Sam felt the knife. In one eye, he saw fireworks. In the other, he watched Del struggle, like she was trying to fork the last peach in a can.

It took eons to complete the task. Severing the optic nerve required a delicate hand. As a surgeon, Del was a much better fuck.

Once the blade gouged the remaining eye, he saw only brightness. Sam imagined this was how Heaven looked.

"Damn, that's good eyeball," Sam heard a pleasant voice say from somewhere north of Wonderland, west of Oz.

"What now?" Sasquatch whispered.

"Now we dump his ass. Load him and Evel in the jeep. We've got to ditch the bodies far from here. He's dripping all over the place. Goddamn tampon. Then come back and give me a hand. I wanna burn some product. How do you think baby brother learned to cook? It will help me think. It's about covering all the bases now. No loose ends."

An eternity later, Sam rose. His world had turned black. In the blackness, a cat lurked, a very big cat. It was a lion wearing a football helmet. The lion spoke in Evel's voice. A Queen song played in the background. The lion spoke.

"You suck. You fucking suck. We're the best. No one is better than us. No one can beat us. We are number one. We're number one. We're number one. We're number one."

The mantra was a broken record in need of smashing.

And then a cartoon mouse swallowed the lion. In a voice that sounded like a swarm of bees, the mouse said, "Damn, that's good lion. You can call me Del."

Sam jerked awake. He was in the jeep. His jeep. He knew its smell, the feel of its worn leather. The hog he rode as a Philistine was just part of the charade, just a heavy metal accessory to complete the character. The jeep he loved; he couldn't part with it, no matter if it was nickel and diming him to death with all the repairs.

Something was on top of him. 180 pounds of jackass he imagined. Or maybe one recently extinct Sasquatch. He wouldn't put it past Del. Nah, smelled too clean to be Sassy. Sam shifted and squirmed, struggled for elbowroom. The weight moved. He could breathe again. Now if only he could free his hands. He strained muscles hardened by years in the gym, a lifetime of weight and resistance training. For all his strength, there was no way to break his duct tape bonds. The bullet in his shoulder didn't help. But with enough leverage, his blood and sweat had made his skin slick. If only, almost, almost, son of a bitch.

One hand slipped free.

He felt his way to the front seat, lifted the divider. Inside were CD's. The inner most CD was Van Halen's *Fair Warning*. It was his favorite; it never left the jeep. Sandwiched between *Fair Warning* and *Diver Down* was a spare key. He'd put it there the last time the jeep was in the shop. Lately, it had always been in the shop so he just left it there for the mechanics to use.

He felt his head, touching bone. His skull was surprisingly warm.

He stuck the key in the ignition, said a prayer and a curse, and turned.

First a sputter.

"Come on baby. Who's my number one bitch?"

Then thunder.

He pressed track five on the CD player and adjusted the volume. Diamond Dave singing "Unchained."

Then an unexpected chorus, "I'm gonna kill that bald bastard for good."

Sam hit the gas targeting the vehicle in the direction of Sasquatch's gunfire.

"Shalom, motherfucker," he shouted.

Sasquatch was the biggest, ugliest bug to ever crack a windshield.

The jeep plowed through Sasquatch and crashed though Alligator Jack's. The gas tank exploded, igniting the meth lab.

Kaboom. No orgasm ever sounded so sweet.

Alligator Jack's fire-balled a second time.

This time, the place burned to the ground.

Three bodies were identified. Del's body was never recovered. Officially, she's a missing person. Unofficially, the Lions had a better chance of winning back-to-back Super Bowls.

The day of the funeral, there wasn't a cloud in the sky. The service was simple and brief. The inscription on the tombstone read, "He lived to serve." As far as happy endings went, Sam would have said it sucked.

STARTING OVER

Have you ever been so close to death you could taste it? Savor it, let it dance on your tongue, roll it around like a fine liqueur before swallowing it down? And you can't wait for the next taste, addict that you are?

Have you ever thought you were going nuts, been so close to madness, you could hear it echo in your skull? Going insane and feeling every step and you can't wait for the next one because you know where it's taking you?

Have you ever hated? I mean really hated, and relied on that hatred to get you through the day? Letting it pick you up, getting you off your knees? Comforting arms embracing you, better than Viagra or any vitamin, more meaningful than any relationship to God, country or your fellow man?

What do you know about love?

I met her while visiting a friend at college. I was graduating the following morning from a different school. You'd think I'd be happy. Not quite. I felt like whatever future I had was reduced to ashes. Just back to my hometown, another fuck up in a town of fuck ups. I just wanted to see my friend and drink. Mainly drink. Who would have guessed I'd meet the love of my life? Funny how things work out.

She lived on the same floor as my friend, a couple door downs. She was introduced as Melissa and that's how she stayed. Her family and friends called her Missy, but she was always Melissa to me. She always will be. I can't honestly say it was love at first sight, but the attraction was certainly there. Like a moth to the flame. I can remember her offering me a bottle. "Have some Jagermeister, little boy." She was my kind of girl. We all went to rent some videos. I remember holding her arm (she was already a little tipsy), her knocking the film *Re-Animator,* me countering her criticisms, me actually having a damn good time because of her.

The movies were forgotten as we engaged in conversation and consumption. I spent the night on the floor in her room, sandwiched between her and her passed-out roommate. It was a really good time.

I left the following morning, going back to my university to finish packing and wait for my ride home. She had to leave for work. We exchanged kisses before we parted like we had throughout the night. They were damn good, sweeter than cotton candy. She was special. I never expected to see her again.

A few months later, with a little prompting from the mutual friend who had introduced us, I sent her a letter, thanking her for such a wonderful evening. She was studying in Germany. A few days after mailing the letter, I received one from Melissa. We had started writing to each other out of the blue. It was like fate or something. I was actually dumb enough to believe that.

Our correspondence blossomed. We grew to know each other and became pen pals if not long-distance friends, talking about bands, films, the wonders of European plumbing, and life and times on planet Earth. We were sharing.

Then she came back to the States. I was the first person she visited. I was nervous, as was she. We went to the zoo, not exactly the most romantic of places. She was wearing all black, a Nirvana T-shirt and Docs. I remember. We made fun of the animals and the uncaged children. Later that night, we watched *The Fisher King*. We kissed to a chorus of crickets. It was even better than I remembered.

We wound up moving in together. I'm not sure whose idea it was, although I'm pretty sure it wasn't mine. She was still living with her dad and her dad's girlfriend who she hated. Me, I had the stereotypical bachelor pad complete with roaches. It wasn't much, but it was home. She never complained.

We lived together for six years. During that time, we fought, partied, cried, fucked and loved. We *lived* together, sharing everything. It was the best time of my life. Funny how things changed.

The change occurred so slowly that I never saw it coming. I never realized what was happening. They say you don't hear the bullet that hits you. I was target practice and didn't know it.

It started with the walks, innocent enough. Then the phone calls. I thought nothing of it. I had no reason to. Then the coming home late. She always had a good excuse. I believed her.

Things went to hell on Valentine's Day. So much for romance. It was like having my heart crushed, squeezing the last drop of emotion out. I never cried like that in my life. I never felt that bad, that hurt, that empty. The pain brought me to my knees. I told her she was my world. It didn't stop her from leaving.

The following days were a blur. I didn't sleep much, maybe two or three hours at best. How could I, without Melissa next to me? I lay there praying she'd come back and if she didn't, praying I wouldn't wake up. Three nights without her, I thought I'd show her. What I needed was to get laid. That's the cure. I went to a bar. It's tough to approach someone when your eyes are full of tears. On the way home, I stopped by a drug store and spent a long time pricing sleeping pills. I wasn't concerned about falling asleep. I was concerned about waking up. I thought of more ways to kill myself, taking a bath with an alarm clock, cutting my wrists. Anything to stop the hurt.

During this time, we still talked. We had to divide our stuff, sort things out financially. I tried to be civil, to be polite. In letters, notes, emails, phone calls, I was insistent on remaining friends, all the while thinking of ways to win her back.

Melissa said she had been staying with Kate, a friend. I took an Easter basket to Kate's with a note saying, "The rabbit left it here by mistake." I knew something was wrong. Melissa's car was nowhere to be seen. My mind was traveling at warp speed, putting the pieces together. Upon arriving home, I called the only other place I thought she'd be, the one place I prayed she wasn't. Melissa answered the phone. I could barely find the words to accuse her of what I thought. She had an excuse, some bullshit about dog sitting. I believed her. I was a fool.

I sent her one last letter, eight pages in length, putting my heart in every line. I thought it would work. I was always better on paper. I wanted it to work. We met, talked, cried and laughed. She finally admitted to fucking around. I still wanted to work things out. I thought she did to. I didn't sleep that night, too many thoughts tap-dancing on my brain.

I called Kate the following morning. Kate said Melissa hadn't come home. I had my answer. Ground glass would have been easier to swallow.

I was blind with anger. I took it out on her car, breaking every window like she had done to my heart. I didn't plan on stopping there. I phoned her, telling her what I had done. I wanted her to press charges. I wanted an excuse, not that I didn't have a good one already. Instead she just cried, telling me how sorry she was. I didn't have any more words for her.

I tore up every photo I had of her, of us together. I threw out all of those Goddamn letters that brought us together in the first place. I listened to a lot of music, songs about love gone bad. There was plenty of material to choose from. I wasn't the first to go through it nor would I be the last. I put my pain into words, line after line of bad poetry, professing my love and loss. It was a form of catharsis, just like breaking her windows. It didn't help. I felt empty, like I'd been hollowed out with a dull knife.

At some point, I thought about how to put my life back together, what *I* needed to do. I went into therapy, talking to the shrink about things I had never told anyone, things dating back to my childhood. I threw myself into my job, working 12-hour days, just to fill time. It got me through. It helped.

It allowed me to think about revenge.

I wanted to not just kill her but kill her entire family. Her dad, her siblings, the nieces and nephews, all of them. Not that I had anything against her family, I just wanted to intensify her suffering. I hoped she'd get a pet just so I could take its life. I wanted to be there to see her as her family died, to watch her suffer as I had suffered.

I was patient. I could wait. It could be months, even years. I'd have my revenge.

I planned to use her credit card. I still had an old receipt and had hoped to rack up a lot of purchases. Nothing I needed or wanted, just something to annoy her. I sent her magazine subscriptions, *Walking, Essence, Vibe, Cosmopolitan,* all things she had no interest in.

I thought about eating her, just so she'd still be part of me.

Sometimes I thought killing would be too good for her. Better to just maim her, cripple her, disfigure her. I wanted to make her so ugly no one would look at her. Children would scream, adults vomit. Taking bites out of her face. Cutting out her eyes. Let her go through life sightless. I imagined cutting her fingers off, one by one. Seal girl.

She always hated snakes. I thought about sending her a boa constrictor for Christmas. Seasons Greetings. Or maybe a letter containing ticks, hoping she'd contract Rocky Mountain spotted fever or Lyme disease. I could only hope. Maybe she'd get pregnant. With sextuplets.

I didn't do any of those things except call her in the middle of the night. If I couldn't sleep, why should she? I knew I was the better person.

And I am the better person, even if it did take months of therapy, thousands of dollars and an endless supply of tears.

One day looking in the mirror, it dawned on me what I had to do. I went to the library and looked up books on the subject. I spent hours on the Internet, finding out everything I could. I spoke with others who had been through it. They tried to talk me out of it.

The hormones took a bit of getting used to. As did the electrolysis. Estrogen doesn't stop hair growth and I had no plans to work in a sideshow next to the seal girl. It was necessary, as was the hip augmentation, the rhinoplasty, and breast enlargement surgery. I'm still not used to having tits.

My coworkers call me Missy, but I always introduce myself as Melissa. Don't get me wrong. There have been drawbacks. I make less than I used to. I spend more time in the bathroom, more time shopping too. Sometimes I miss having a penis. But it was worth it. Sometimes people mistake me for her.

I have better legs, firmer tits, a tighter ass, and fuller lips. I'm better than her, morally, physically. I'm beautiful. I look in the mirror and know that as truth. The reflection does not lie.

THE PSYCHIC

The photo failed to do him justice. Captured inno-
cence; curly brown hair, dimples, the beginnings of a
frown suggesting growing impatience at remaining still
too long. A third grader whose favorite things were Spi-
der-man, mashed potatoes and fishing trips with his
grandpa. The coroner snapped another photo. Special
Agent Alex Wilkerson stared at the photo, then at the
body partially covered by dirt and black garbage bags.
He never got use to it. The face in the shallow grave
looked unreal, more like a prop from a low-budget horror film than someone's son.

The scraps of skin that remained had been stretched
taunt. The color of dried mustard. It was easy to see the
cause of death. A fist-sized hole had splintered the skull.
Wilkinson had a moment of déjà vu. The other five
bodies possessed similar wounds, cause of death reported as blunt head trauma. Most likely a claw hammer. The owner of the weapon was still at large.

Wilkerson stared at the corpse, at the tiny curls
decorating the skull. He had no doubt the corpse in the
ground was Toby Jordan. Just where the psychic said
he would be. Now they just had to find the twin sister,
also missing, and he could get the hell out of here.

*   *   *

Thunderclouds circled the sky above the trailer. Inside, the storm had already passed. The psychic sat with her bourbon and Coke, the headache behind her temples subsiding. She knew they had found Toby. That news would push the mother, already a basket case, over the edge. Her biggest joy had been her kids; now they were gone. The father was not even an afterthought. No name on the birth certificate, no photos. Just a kind face in the lonely hours of need, only a shadow. Pity. In cases of homicide, the psychic knew young victims were likely to have known their aggressor. She had mentioned that to Agent Wilkerson. She liked Alex. He was a good man, had a bit of cowboy in him. She knew the sorrow he still felt over the affair that caused his divorce, the guilt every time he kissed his new wife goodbye. Finding the body was a small victory; it was the hands behind the murders he wanted. She had a drink, tasting the bourbon. She hoped to oblige him.

*   *   *

Carlos Molina was concerned. He didn't know the woman across the street very well; they were just nodding neighbors but she seemed friendly enough. Liz was her name. He knew that much from the news. Liz mostly kept to herself but sometimes her kids played with his, during his custodial weekends. They seemed like good kids, quick to smile. The girl liked strawberry ice cream. She laughed at his accent. He spoke Spanish just to hear her laugh.

A tear rolled down his cheek. He prayed for the girl, her mother. He prayed for the boy. He prayed for his own kids, that they remain safe. He prayed for himself, that the dreams would stop. The nightmares left him shaking, a scream trapped behind his lips. Images played at the corners of perception, like scrapbook photos caught in a whirlwind. Images that he couldn't place. He was scared too.

As he left for work, a car rolled up. Police, he figured. He nodded as he stepped behind the wheel of the ice cream truck. In the mirror, watching as they headed to the house opposite his, he breathed a sigh of relief.

*　　*　　*

The headache had returned. The bourbon wasn't helping. She was getting too old for this. She looked at her collection of news articles. She often woke in the middle of night to read them. Some mentioned her by name.

Agent Wilkerson would arrive soon. She would congratulate him on his find. Two in one day. She would offer him a drink. She thought he would accept. And then, staring into those sad blue eyes, a few more small details about the killer. He has an accent she'll say. A smell of vanilla. Such a tease.

She touched the hammer to her forehead; cold steel offered little relief. Another statistic came to mind. Men made up 90% of the world's total serial killers. She wondered if Agent Wilkerson knew that. She bet he did.

THE SAMARITAN

Licorice hated winter. Always had. He remembered as a kid waiting for the school bus, freezing his ass off, his face going numb. Later as a teenager, walking to school was even worse. Sitting in class in wet shoes and wet clothes. The dampness was bad enough but the real humiliation came from his classmates. No one said anything to his face but he remembered the giggles. Punching girls wasn't going to move him any higher on the high school social ladder. He was always somehow closer to the bottom rung than the top. At least the school was warm. At home, he would wake, his breath visible. Not that Mom was even close to being rich, but they could afford the extra heat. She was afraid the furnace would explode if she turned it up. It failed to explode when she was gone, and Licorice cranked it up. You couldn't explain that to her.

After his divorce, the holidays never meant as much. He spent them alone, on the road, traveling from one job to the next. He always hated shopping, the glut of humanity infected with consumerism, looking to find the perfect gift at a bargain price. It was madness. He still avoided malls and crowds as much as possible. He despised both the cold and the snow. One or the other was bad enough, but the combination was the worst. People said they loved winter. Shit for brains. They must be loving it today, at least a foot of snow on the ground already and more to come according to the latest forecast. Just so much fun to drive in. Stupid fucks. He had already passed at least a dozen cars stuck in the snow.

He was making good time. The Expedition wasn't having much trouble with the weather so far. He wasn't accustomed to driving a vehicle this large. Licorice adapted quick. As confident as the SUV's size made him feel, there was no reason to get stupid. He couldn't afford a fender bender or wind up in a ditch. He had only passed one snowplow so far. The city workers had a long night ahead of them.

Damn. He almost missed his exit. Visibility was bad. Only a fool would be out in weather like this. He was a fool on business. The radio said a snow emergency had been declared. They were going through the school closings now. He remembered his daughter, Lisa, listening to the radio, hugging it close as if proximity would guarantee at least an hour delay. Lisa loved school but like most kids, she enjoyed the unexpected day off. He remembered helping her build her first snowman. Pop cans for eyes, a beer bottle for a nose. It took days to melt. Lisa was like an Eskimo; you had to force her back inside. She could pack a mean snowball, too. She loved winter, must have gotten it from her mom.

He skimmed the radio dial. Nothing worth a damn. His own school days were less than memorable. It's amazing how much crap accumulated in childhood and adolescence stuck with you into adulthood. Static cling from hell. Christ, more people knew him by his nickname than the one on his birth certificate. Licorice. Kevin Miller started that shit in third grade because of his wardrobe. His mother bought him dark clothes. She said dirt didn't show as much. Black shirts. Black pants.

Black socks. It looked like he was in constant morning, which was true in a sense. Today it's fashionable but back then it was the catalyst for playground fights. Miller got his too. A black eye.

In his mirror, Licorice saw flashing lights. He checked his speed, well under the limit. The lights drew nearer, two car lengths behind him now, and then passed to another lane. Just a salt truck.

He saw a sign for the Mt. Airy Nature Preserve. He checked his watch. Quarter after eleven. It wouldn't be long now. The Preserve was created in 1911 when the local park board purchased 168 acres of land, starting the first municipal reforestation project in the United States. The preserve was now 1,471 acres. Big enough to lose yourself. A good thing. He wasn't in the mood for company tonight.

Reducing his speed, he turned into the park entrance. Most of the signs were obscured by snow. He knew where he was going. He had been in the area for a few days before the snowfall, doing some sightseeing. Licorice believed in preparation.

He passed a snow-covered picnic area. Post card perfect. Icicles dangled from tree limbs, frozen stalactites beautiful in their imperfection. Another turn and a softball field came into view. It was as good a place as any. He put the Expedition in park and got out. He looked like a shadow given substance. Some things never change. Snow spilled into his black boots. Something caught his eye. Movement off to his right.

He thought it might be a deer. A brochure he picked up said deer inhabited the forest. But the shape was too low to the ground to be any type of deer unless it was some type of pygmy. The shape stopped. Licorice walked towards it, hoping for a better look when the shape sprinted forward. It was fast, covering ground like it was floating while he struggled not to trip. Ten feet. Nine. He wiped the snow from his face to get a better look. Eight feet. Jesus Christ, it was a wolf.

It wasn't actually a wolf, although it was hairy enough and had the chompers to pass. It was a Keeshound. An old neighbor had one. Thor. Playful dog, although Thor liked to bark. A lot. Especially at 6 a.m. on the weekends. Lisa loved that dog so much that he got her a dog of her own. A dachshund named Oscar. Lisa came up with the name. She would ask Thor's owner if he and Oscar could play. They chased each other around like Wile E. Coyote and the Roadrunner. They'd wrestle, too. He laughed watching the wiener dog wrestle the much larger Thor to the ground. Oscar was one of the things he missed the most after the divorce. But what was this dog doing here now?

None of his research showed that anyone actually lived on the park's ground. There were no residential properties for miles. So why was this dog running loose? The dog didn't look very old, but he was hardly an expert. It kept a safe distance. No collar but a lot of pet owners had their pets microchipped these days. If he could just catch the damn thing. Somebody probably just dumped it in the woods. Exit one Christmas present. His ex carried an extra leash in her car just in case she happened on a stray. He had no idea where the nearest shelter was located. He didn't really have time to chase some fucking dog either. But he couldn't just leave it out here to freeze.

The dog watched, ears on full alert, like it was waiting for something. He approached it, palm outstretched. Nothing to fear here, boy. Suddenly, the dog darted back into the woods. He ran after it, tripped and fell face-first into the snow. Fuck. He hated this time of year.

"Here pooch, here poochie," he called. The dog stood watching. He moved in its direction, slower this time. Just as he got close, the dog took off like it was training for the Iditarod. Fucking great time to be playful. He walked back to the truck, weighing his options.

The dog barked. For a medium-sized dog, it sounded like a werewolf. Christ! It just keeps getting better, he thought. He climbed into the truck and started the engine.

The Expedition reversed out of the snow-covered parking lot. He decided to head back towards the entrance. The dog followed. He traveled slowly, making sure he didn't lose sight of the dog. When the dog disappeared from his line of sight, he stopped. The dog barked. It was a game.

He saw a few grills, looking like frozen midgets. He had some idea where he was. But the dog, just like that, was gone. He stopped. Silence. He stepped out of the truck. Still nothing.

"Goddamn. Stupid fucking dog, where are you?"

He walked around the truck. The dog had disappeared. He didn't have time for this. Licorice started the truck, intending to finish the evening's original plan. He headed back towards the field, still looking for the dog. Suddenly, his rear passenger wheel began to spin. No fucking way was he getting stuck. He floored it.

"Come on, baby. A little more and we're there. Come on fucker."

The truck lurched forward.

Thump.

This can't be happening. A fur-covered shape lay still in the headlights. It raised its head as he approached, licked his gloved hand. The dog was in bad shape, blood dripping from its snout, panting for breath. It tried to wag its tail. Man's best friend to the end.

He had no idea where the nearest vet would be. Licorice couldn't stand to see an animal suffer.

He patted its head. "Poor dog." He dug into his coat, pulling out a late Christmas present. It was a .38.

"Good dog, good boy."

He put a bullet in its brain.

He pulled a garbage bag from the truck. The dog weighed about 25 pounds. He had never killed a dog before and prayed he never had to again. Enough of this Old Yeller shit.

Wiping a tear from his eye, he loaded the corpse into the truck.

He drove the short distance to the softball field. He turned the engine off. Time to end this now. Snow continued to fall. He said aloud, "No wonder suicide rates soar this time of year. It's fucking depressing." He opened the rear door. One tug and a large object dropped to the ground. He dragged his other late Christmas gift, custom-wrapped in duct tape and curtains, to home plate.

His present to himself couldn't move, hands and feet hog-tied. His present couldn't speak; the gag was still in place, like some S/M bow. His present was named Jimmy Barns and Mr. Barns had two major character flaws: a big mouth and a fondness for young girls. Both were proving to be costly. He'd already lost his gun, his truck and received a dent in his forehead courtesy of said gun. All for some underage cooze.

Jimmy's biggest mistake to date had been his involvement with Licorice's daughter, Lisa. The two met when Lisa was twelve. Jimmy was her softball coach.

Where did the blame belong? The community for allowing Jimmy's continued involvement with anything involving minors. They had heard the rumors. Lisa's mother for allowing her daughter to end up thirteen and pregnant? Hadn't she taught her daughter about birth control or safe sex or don't fuck people twice your age? Lisa for being a little girl who found a replacement father figure to show her love and affection? Lisa's father for not being there?

When he learned of Lisa's suicide, Licorice blamed himself. When he found out she had been pregnant, he started asking questions.

As a pro, Licorice didn't have that many contacts, preferring anonymity to friends with loose lips. He'd seen too many guys go to the grave due to that flaw. Fortunately, he had a few outstanding favors. This time it was more than business, more than just personal; it was family.

Jimmy was gift-wrapped. The gag still in place kept him from begging, pleading or denying. Blood had coagulated on his forehead like smeared cranberry sauce. Licorice imagined this fuck sticking his dick in his daughter. She looked so much older in the casket.

Licorice took off his leather coat, his designer gloves. He needed room to swing. The baseball bat felt like an old friend. A graphite/titanium blend. Light, durable and very little vibration. It was time for the old friend to make a new acquaintance.

The ground had turned red. It reminded him of a Cherry slush, Lisa's favorite. He was starting to sweat. He was just warming up.

"Auld Lang Syne" played on the radio. He always hated that song. His back hurt from loading the garbage bags into the truck. Must have pulled a muscle. He didn't know what he was going to do with the dog's body. Licorice turned the knob, found a country station. Johnny Cash was singing about a woman in a black veil. The snow continued to fall.

SELLING SEA SHELLS

Sally couldn't believe her luck. This was her fourth shell of this type today. It was a queen conch. She traced the beautiful, intricate spiral pattern with her fingers. The bigger shells sold for more money, especially if they were fully intact, to the tourists who were too lazy to comb the beaches themselves. This one was complete, no missing pieces. Brushing the sand from the conch with her fingertips, her latest discovery was at least eight inches in length, a respectable-sized shell for this type of conch.

The smaller shells she used to design jewelry. Her necklaces proved to be highly popular and were big sellers with the tourists, too.

This stretch of beach was a veritable treasure chest of shells: olives, cones, murex, Venus clams and more. All former homes were now abandoned, the former residents most likely food for something else. Sometimes the occupant, or at least parts of the occupant, remained.

At her home, Sally would soak the shells in a bleach-and-water solution, making sure to remove the periostracum, the flaky leathery layer that covered most live seashells. After bleaching, barnacles and other matter would be removed using a toothbrush and some gentle scrubbing or a dental pick for the more stubborn pieces.

She would then shine them with baby oil, giving them a luster sure to attract the tourists' eyes.

Sally loved the beach, always had. It was in her blood. The smell of the salt air, watching gulls dive for food, the tiny crabs, smaller than a quarter, playing hide-and-seek in the sand. This was thunderstorm season. She loved watching lightning streak across the skies, like the heavens were cracking. At night, there was no separation between sea and sky. Dual moons stared at each other across the void, like strangers watching and waiting for the other to move. They were dancers, forever apart, yet forever in synch.

Pelicans skimmed the blue water like skipping stones as Sally pocketed the conch in her bag and continued her trek up the beach. She took her sandals off, letting the sand cascade over her toes. The sand kept her feet soft and smooth. People paid good money for the type of dermabrasion the beach offered at no charge. The incoming tide tickled her toes and washed away her footprints, leaving no trace of her path.

A cormorant darted beneath the waves, looking for a breakfast of fish, eel or perhaps a sea snake. A few seconds later, it surfaced, shaking water from its feathered crest. Shampoo-like foam formed on the beach. Sally watched rays, like floating pancakes, ride the incoming tides.

She loved this time of day, early morning, the beach largely deserted save for the native wildlife or the vacationing early bird, determined to run a few laps before succumbing to the flavor of local food and drink. Sometimes she would catch a glimpse of dolphins or, even more rare, whales, with one fin turned upright like they were waving. She always felt compelled to wave back. She was reminded of the lines from the Stevie Smith poem:

"I was much further out than you thought
And not waving but drowning."

Her mother had once taught English, and Sally inherited her mother's love of verse, as well as her features: long, dark hair and exotic good looks, a reflection of her mixed Mexican-European ancestry. The British poem had been one of her favorites.

Her father, long since disappeared in the waves of time, hailed from Massachusetts by way of Polperro, a small fishing village on the Cornwall coast in southwest England. From him, Sally inherited her love of the sea, she supposed. She really had no memories of him, save for an old black-and-white photo of a smiling, handsome man holding a stringer full of mahi-mahi.

She remembered her mother reading her bedtime stories like The Nahuales, people who could transform into animals, and Dos Lagunas, the two lagoons, the tale of Leubo, son of the water god, cursed to be together and apart with his human lover Flor. The lovers were both transformed by a witch into two huge lagoons forever divided by a strip of solid land. When she had been especially naughty, her mother scared her with stories of *La Llorona*, the floating woman, who appeared wherever there was running water, looking for her own children whom she had killed and thrown into the sea, like discarded, forgotten toys.

As a child, she dreamed of scaled creatures, crawling from the black depths looking for children. Nightmarish, tentacled things with translucent eyes and unnaturally white bellies like a dead man's skin. Some forgotten, prehistoric horror swimming her way, up from the murky depths, tapping on aquarium glass. She had American horror films to thank for such nightmares.

She imagined what the Gillman would be doing now, with his predilection for Caucasian females. Probably lending his face to selling boxed, preprocessed fish sticks.

Such thoughts were better lost in childhood.

Her stand, where she sold her shells on the boardwalk, the *Malecón*, was sandwiched between makers of homemade candy like Peanut Marzaipan, Mango Pops, colorful sugar skulls and cinnamon-filled cookies and the one-eyed artist Manuel, who painted orange cartoon cats into all his works.

Manuel, born in Los Cabos, was a huge fan of American gangsta rap and was always dressed in images of his icons. T-shirts of Nas, the Wu-Tang Clan, Tupac and Ice-T dominated his fashion sense, along with low-slung, brief-displaying jeans. He lost the eye due to choroidal melanoma, a serious cancer within the eye. When questioned about the pirate patch, in order to maintain his street cred, he claimed he was the victim of a drug deal gone bad. In truth, if you were in need of some local herb or other pharmaceutical, Manuel was the hook up. There was no question about that; he knew all the local farmers and budding chemists.

Around the corner stood city hall with its sprawling murals of peasants tending their crops, sailboats shadowed by feathered, flying gods and skeletal Mariachi bands decorating the walls and ceilings. It also had a tiled starfish pool in the lobby, each tile painstakingly painted. It served as a wishing well. Pesos and international currency sank like forgotten treasures. Sadly, no record of its accuracy was maintained.

One of the local churches, the Shrine to Our Lady of Sorrow, stood in the immediate distance. The church's centerpiece, a huge golden globe supported by eight stone angels, could be seen throughout most of down-town.

Sally knew that extra pesos passed through certain elected officials' hands, ensuring that tour guides would lead their buses full of visitors right through the heart of commerce. There was also a steady swarm of taxis, dropping people off, like ants delivering food to the nest. It was a constant supply of consumers and the *Malecón*, full of crafts, food, a variety of tequila and mezcal (complete with worm or scorpion depending on the drinker's preference), *Lucha Libre* wrestling masks and T-shirts every color of the rainbow, welcomed them all with open arms.

Recently, there had been much talk about the development of a floating casino. In all likelihood, town council would grease the wheels of progress. New jobs would benefit the community, but Sally wondered if long-term effects would have a detrimental impact. She failed to see how an increase in pawnshops and the futile dream of instant riches would be positive for the surrounding neighborhoods. She could remember tales from her mother of how the local graveyard grew as the city's populace declined, when the fishermen's nets went dry. Hard times met by even harder sacrifices.

Sally's stand at the market was close to local sculptures, which presented great photo opportunities. Visitors could sit in bronze-colored thrones crowned with squids and octopuses with humanoid feet and a surrealist's version of scuba. There was also the ladder of triangular-headed priests, an evolutionary ladder undreamed by Darwin, but undeniably photogenic.

Here she would entertain tourists with tales of local history, dining suggestions, directions to the weekly bullfights and afterhours fun, all the while displaying her wares. Her shell-encrusted, handcrafted crucifixes were surprisingly popular items; she couldn't create them fast enough to meet the demand.

Like any intelligent businesswoman, she had business cards with her printed phone number. She handed them to men whose eyes lingered more on her than her jewelry. Sally had learned a lingering touch, lack of a bra and a smile full of promise proved to be more efficient selling points than any marketing class could teach.

On occasion, a curious tourist would offer to buy her dinner, wanting to sample more of the local cuisine outside of what was offered at their all inclusive-resort hotel. Male or female, Sally wasn't one to turn down a free meal; she relished the chance to dine at Le Kliff, with its spectacular ocean view or Kuma, known for their mouth-watering seafood. And if dinner turned to dancing, well, it was very convenient she was on a first-name basis with the doormen at Diva, D'Santos, Zoo, La Iguana or the Kit Kat Club with its leopard skin décor.

And if dancing turned to something more, Sally knew of numerous, discreet locations on the beach where one could linger without the intrusion of prying eyes.

She had entertained a gentleman not far from the spot where she acquired the conch shell, the preceding evening. After a night of drinking and dancing, the gentleman, a credit card machine salesman from the midwestern United States, suggested a moonlight stroll. Sally knew the perfect spot.

The signs said "Swim at your own risk." She couldn't recall news of any recent drownings or shark attacks. There was greater risk of getting hit by one of the taxi's chasing fares to and from the airport.

He talked about his job, how hard it was to meet women, how beautiful her eyes were. He asked about her name. Sally didn't sound Spanish. She explained that it translated as savior. He grinned. The American was lost in the rapture of her flesh. Tenderly, he kissed her cleavage, all the while grinding his erection against her pelvis.

Sally and her companion were caught up in the moment. Clothes were shed without discretion. Sam, the salesman, entered her with a condom-covered thrust. Both of them were lost in the rhythm, lost in each other. She imagined ghostly pirate ships and a mermaids fashion show, wedding dresses decorated in kelp.

Sam didn't feel the tentacles encircling his legs, didn't feel the dentides, small-tooth like scales, sinking into his flesh. By then, Sally had already inserted the dental pick into his aorta; she couldn't bear to see any living creature in pain.

Sally knew the beach like the palm of her hand; a secret knowledge born of hours of personal trespass and almost forgotten ancestry. It was in her blood. No one heard the screams. No one ever heard the screams. A loud splash then a gurgle. Sally thought of whelks, gastropods equipped with an extensible proboscis, tipped with a file-like radula, ribbons of teeth used to bore holes through the shells of clams, crabs and lobsters. Human flesh proved to be much less resistant.

Further up the beach, she discovered a piece of leather. It smelled of seaweed. Inside the mammal-turned-wallet, she found an ample amount of U.S. currency, her own business card, and photos of, she assumed, friends and family of Sam's.

She thought of the empty crib at home. Life was about sacrifice. Her own child, fathered by a featureless tourist, and offered up for adoption, in hopes of a better life.

The coral king always paid his debts. The waves, silent and constant, seemed to nod their approval. Sally agreed, pocketed the wallet's contents, and walked on.

THE BETTER
MOUSETRAP

He hoped a move to the suburbs would allow him the privacy his work demanded. Given a choice, he would have preferred the country, scenic surroundings and no nosing neighbors, but his allergies would never allow it. Fresh air and a high pollen count sent him gasping and grasping for his inhaler. Smog alerts be damned. At least here, in his three-bedroom, two-story townhouse, he could breathe easily.

Wilbur Frankensmith placed the black garbage bag inside a cardboard box that once contained unbreakable glass beakers. Wilbur found that not only did the beakers break, they tended to shatter. He noted that in his complaint letter to the manufacturer. Beakers didn't come cheap. Box in hand, he briskly walked the path to his twin garbage cans, but not too briskly. He didn't wish to call any undue attention to himself. Over the years, he had perfected the art of blending. His religion was the art of camouflage. He considered himself an expert, not that anyone would notice. But that was the whole point.

Across the driveway, movement behind a curtain caught his eye. The widow Romanello was a retired teacher. Wilbur had learned that fact when he was unfortunate enough to be trapped by one of her conversations. She liked to putter around with her plants, and was an amateur bird watcher. She wore her binoculars like a status symbol. Professional snoop with too much time on her wrinkled hands, more like it. Wilbur forced his hand to wave, hoping she wouldn't take it as an invitation to impose her mundane observations or recipes for bread pudding on him. She didn't. Thank God. She just waved back.

He waited until he was sure she had moved on, and then, as if he were crossing a busy intersection, he looked both ways and behind him, and once more just in case he missed any prying eyes. Satisfied, Wilbur placed the box and its contents inside the trashcan. He was attacked by the smell. What a stink! Wilbur hoped the garbage strike wouldn't last much longer. Oh well, another failure now out of sight, but not out of mind.

With the lid secured by a brick and satisfied, this simple domestic act had called no attention to himself, Wilbur pulled up his pants and made sure his white shirt was tucked in. After re-buttoning his red-splotched lab coat, he quickly—but not too quickly—retreated to the quiet sanctuary of his home.

Silent as the shadows concealing it, a pair of eyes watched everything. Their owner's only expression was the motion of its tail, back and forth like a snake waiting for the moment to strike.

Inside, Wilbur paused to plug in his mechanical assistant. The Intelligence-Guided Organizational Robot, or IGOR for short, was a great housekeeper, but had a horrible tendency to run down after a few hours of operation, which was the main reason the model was discontinued by NASA. Still, the increase in the electric bill was worth it. Wilbur hated doing laundry.

He stripped off the lab coat and washed his hands. Wilbur hesitated only briefly before grabbing a wine cooler. Calypso Colada was his favorite; he loved the hint of coconut. He convinced himself one bottle would be OK. He deserved it. Drink in hand, he plopped himself into his state-of-the-art Power Recliner 5000. The chair was a gift from a friend in the military. It came complete with a refrigerated drink holder with vibrating action (which, when set on high, caused soda to fizz) and included a hidden compartment for firearms. Wilbur hid snacks in there. He sipped his drink, played with his ponytail, and waited for *Jeopardy* to come on the tube. Wilbur prided himself on always getting at least 80.78% of the answers correct. Developing a buzz, he thought about the only thing he thought about these days: his greatest success... and failure.

*   *   *

After stints working for NASA, the Pentagon and a few jobs in the private sector, Wilbur decided to return to the family business—research. Of course, research needed funding and, even with the benefit of Spell Check, as a grant writer Wilbur made a much better mad scientist. Fortunately for him, some of his previous inventions paid off. His patent for flavorless gum for people who just like to chew, while not a huge money-maker, helped pay the bills. It didn't hurt that it was also useful for fixing flats and sticking things to walls.

He remembered family talks about the old days; times when, if you needed fresh specimens, you just visited the local cemetery and commenced digging, back before the change in surname. Like you could ever be taken seriously with that last name. Joe Hitler had a better chance at becoming a moil than Wilbur did a scientist. Dr. Frankensmith had an austere ring to it. The world had changed, progressed. Now with cloning and gene-splicing mentioned on the nightly news, the availability of subjects was just a mouse click away. If you had the money.

For most of his research work, Wilbur relied on a mail-order shop called Corpses and Stuff. While their inventory might not be the freshest, they stood by their product, no matter how bad the smell.

Wilbur's main branch of research dealt with slowing down the aging process. Nobody wants to get old, let alone look his or her age. It occurred to Wilbur that most animals don't show their age the way humans do. What's an old fly or worm or platypus look like? Plus animal corpses were much cheaper than human remains.

Wilbur believed an enzyme in a cat's saliva could invigorate skin cells, giving an 80-year-old woman the skin of a teenager. To capture time—that was the better mousetrap. Cats spent much of their time licking themselves, and hardly seemed to age at all. Not only did the theory seem plausible to Wilbur, but also highly marketable. Once an ad agency got behind the idea, Wilbur would be rolling in dough, instead of clipping coupons. He would be contributing to the good of humanity, too. And while a Nobel Prize might not be in his future, he fantasized about the long line of women waiting to try his miracle product; women who would be willing to show their gratitude to their benefactor in a variety of ways and positions.

This type of thinking was the catalyst for Wilbur's problems.

Possessing multiple degrees, a high IQ and the ability to say, "I love you" in twelve languages didn't mean much, if you didn't have someone to hear the words. Wilbur was lonely. With his work, he didn't have much time to commit to the logical pursuit of companionship. And playing chess with IGOR didn't count.

Like other hopeless romantics and the truly desperate, Wilbur turned to online dating. He had long, typed conversations with Wild1 before actually meeting her at a local coffee shop. She called him "Stallion" because of his hair. Wild1 was everything he had hoped for, and more. It was the "more" that broke his heart. Wild1 turned out to be a pre-op transsexual and, as fascinated as he was from a biological point of view, Wilbur just couldn't come to grips with the situation. He learned that the hard way when he gripped Wild1's penis. "Stallion" bolted for the door like a Kentucky Derby winner.

Rain struck his face as he fled that night. Another date that ended in disaster. Lightning cracked the sky, a wound with jagged edges just like Wilbur's heart. He drove home from Wild1's apartment and proceeded to do something he never did: drink heavily.

He opened a wine cooler, Green Applelicious, spiked with his own special non-FDA approved chemical additive, and got righteously blitzed. Once his head was sufficiently spinning, Wilbur stumbled down to the basement lab. Portraits of his idols watched his descent: Dr. Pretorius, Dr. Jekyll, Dr. Moreau, Dr. Seuss and his own ancestors. In his drunken wisdom, he had an idea, a real breakthrough, he thought.

Nestled between the washer and dryer stood what Wilbur needed. He staggered to the freezer and took out several bottles of brightly colored liquids. He grabbed a plastic bag. Opening the bag, he laid the feline body on the table. The corpse had long, thick gray hair, except for its white feet; it looked like it was wearing socks. Part of an ear was missing, as though predator and prey had switched roles and a bird got a beak full of fur. The stomach had been shaved bare. Stitches stood out like some weird form of Braille. The cat, once beautiful in life, looked like a Halloween prop.

"Good kitty, kitty. Meow. Oh, what a good pussy you are, what a good patient. Wait right here."

Wilbur stroked the freezer-burnt fur and tugged on a whisker, before turning his attention elsewhere.
He proceeded to mix the various liquids from the freezer in a blender. The machine roared to life as thunder boomed outside. Pouring some of the liquid into a centrifuge, he set the device on low, a whirling 5000 RPMs. He poured the separated contents into a beaker.

"Screw romance. Here's to science."

He raised his toast and threw it back.

Wilbur gagged. The liquid burned all the way down. His eyes bugged in cartoon fashion. One large vein on his forehead began to throb. His sweat glands activated. His breath came in pants, like a pervert in need of a phone.

"Damn, that's good."

He had another drink. Before long, the blender was empty. Between gulps, Wilbur conducted his experiments. He knew this because—when he woke up on the floor, his head feverish like a nuclear meltdown and his stomach feeling like dinosaur hide—the dead cat had disappeared.

He scoured the basement like a lepidopterist in search of a rare butterfly, with zero results. After a prolonged visit to the bathroom, Wilbur enlisted IGOR's aid. Both of them yielded nothing, although Wilbur did find religion, vowing to never drink again, so help him,

Intelligent Creator. Wilbur lay down to rest, leaving IGOR to clean up the mess.

Later that night, he first heard it. Unsuccessful at sleeping off his hangover, Wilbur performed chemical equations in his head. He was calculating the formula to change calcium fluoride and sulfuric acid into hydrofluoric acid when he heard the sound. He thought it was IGOR, but IGOR was in the basement, his charge probably long dead.

Wilbur's bedroom was on the second floor. The noise coming from the foot of the bed, like the sound of little motors in motion, wasn't mechanical at all; it was purring. Wilbur moved as fast as his hangover would allow, flipping on his lunar-powered night light just in time to see a bushy tail disappear around the corner.

Wilbur peered down the dark hallway. When he flipped on the hall light, he saw...nothing. Down the steps he went, searching every room, but no sign of the tail. The basement was empty, save for IGOR.

Sitting in the recliner, he wondered if he imagined the whole thing. Sleep that night was restless; the snores loud, drowning out the scratching noises that came from behind the recliner.

Wilbur woke feeling much better. He glanced at the carpet.

"Could use a shampoo," Wilbur thought. "Better include that in IGOR's programming."

He took a closer look at the carpet.

That wasn't dirt.

Cat hair.

It wasn't a dream. In fact, as the impact of events hit him like gravity affecting mass, relatively speaking, he realized it was the best thing to ever happen to him, save for the hangover. Now if he could only recreate it.

He flew into the lab, skipping breakfast and bath. He tried to recreate his actions from last night. Was it two ounces or three? Is the pH right? What's wrong with the formula? Is that blood or just spilled Bloody Mary?

With three soggy cat corpses, one partially dissolved tadpole and six unbreakable beakers broken against the wall, Wilbur was near tears. Growing desperate, he had even given one of the tabbies a chemical bath, hooked it up to a car battery and succeeded only in blackening his fingertips. He just couldn't remember. His only hope was to catch the cat. Once the corpse stopped smoking, he gathered it and the others, securing the remains tightly, and dumped the carcasses in the trash before hopping in his van. He checked his rearview mirror, watching for moving curtains and hidden binoculars.

Wilbur returned from the grocery with a variety of cat food: chicken, veal, tuna, shrimp, salmon and even liver. Wilbur wasn't taking chances. He opened the cans and waited.

Days later, the cans were still open, untouched and starting to smell. Wilbur had retreated to his bedroom to watch through IGOR's surveillance eye, just in case the cat was a finicky eater that couldn't abide being watched. Not a whisker was to be seen.

"Maybe the cat likes more of a challenge."

Newly determined, Wilbur returned from the pet store with a mouse, a hamster, a pair of parakeets and a bag of goldfish. It was buy one, get one free on goldfish.

Wilbur thought the mouse looked the most appetizing. It was the first to taste freedom, promptly voided its nervous bladder and then disappeared behind the kitchen stove.

Always thinking, Wilbur took a wad of his flavorless gum, fashioned a collar, tied it to microfilament cable and placed it around one of the birds. The parakeet began pecking at the gum and turned stiff minutes later. Who knew the stuff was toxic to birds?

Wilbur dumped all the fish into a bowl. They commenced flopping. Time passed; still no cat. The flopping ended; all fins were motionless. Wilbur was running out of animals. Back to the laboratory.

He decided he was going about this wrong. He had to think like a cat. Licking his hand and scratching his ear, he began smearing the untouched cat food on the hamster; a dab of tuna here, a touch of liver there. He decided to set the hamster loose in the lab, thinking the cat could be trapped more easily there.

Back upstairs, the mouse had evidently gotten bored with the scenery beneath the stove and ventured forth. Only the hind legs and tail remained. The cat, eyes like small moons, was using IGOR as a scratching post. A small pink tongue licked furry lips.

Wilbur was amazed. With clinical interest, he watched it breathe in and out. The cat (surely it was the same animal once sprawled on his dissecting table; he could see the stomach scar) yawned with the detachment of a Hollywood star burdened by his fame.

"Here kitty, good kitty. Meow."

Wilbur inched his way closer. The cat watched with a look of perplexity, as if to say, "What in the hell do you think you're doing?"

Wilbur reached out and was greeted with stinging pain. This cat still had its claws, and knew how to use them. Before he was finished cursing, the cat had disappeared, moving with an unnatural grace.

After cleaning and bandaging his wounds and disposing of the dead pets, Wilbur pondered his options. He thought briefly about calling a pest-control expert, going as far as looking up the number of the Critter Getter before deciding it was a bad idea. It just wasn't worth the risk of injuring the animal or, worse, setting it loose. The cat was more than just the sum of its stitches. It definitely preferred live food. But there was no way he was going to risk getting close to those miniature meat hooks again.

"Hmmm," Wilbur purred, stroking his damaged hand.

He tried forcing the surviving parakeet to swallow sedatives. The cat would eat the bird and fall sound asleep. Granted, there was no logic to his plan, but there wasn't anything logical about a dead cat tearing up his furniture, either. The back of the Power Recliner 5000 was in tatters.

The plan failed miserably. The poor bird died of a drug overdose. As evident by the untouched feathers, the cat wasn't a carrion eater. To make matters worse, IGOR accidentally squished the food-smeared hamster in the lab.

"Live bait works best," became Wilbur's credo.

After several more trips to the pet store and, subsequently, the garbage can, Wilbur decided on a new strategy. He adopted a cat. The Burmese was adorable with deep gold eyes and a walnut-colored coat. The love story he was hoping for ended in tragedy. He had never heard a catfight, much less witnessed one. The sounds made him think of a bootleg Roswell video he had seen; immigrants from space engaged in sexual encounters with humans. The sounds of their orgasms haunted him for weeks. And the aliens were just creepy. But that was tame compared to this. Never had he heard such ferocity.

Fleeing from the fight, the Burmese suddenly turned on Wilbur, and a mouthful of small knifes sank into the soft flesh of his already wounded hand. He reacted without thinking. It was self-defense. It still sickened him, the sound of the small bones cracking. That was the latest trip to the garbage.

He sipped his wine cooler, wincing at the pain in his palm. Lost in his thoughts, he had forgotten Jeopardy was on. The contestant buzzed in.

"Who is Bast?"

"I knew that," Wilbur said aloud.

He heard another type of buzzing, one he was not accustomed to. The doorbell rang again.

Two police officers stood on his step, looking very official.

"Evening, officers. Something wrong?"

Wilbur glanced behind him, making sure the cat wasn't eyeing an exit.

The shorter of the two said, "I'm Officer Stern, and this is Officer Tacit."

Officer Tacit nodded his head.

"Are you..." a pause as Officer Stern looked at his note pad, "Frankensmith?"

"Yes, sir. I'm Dr. Frankensmith."

"If that's your van, the tags are expired. But that's not why we're here. There's been a complaint. About the smell."

"What smell?"

Officer Tacit sniffed the air. One whiff and he detected the source. The cop walked toward the garbage cans, one hand near his pistol, the other gripping his nose.

"I'd say the smell's coming from over there."

Peripheral movement caught Wilbur's attention. Glancing sideways, he saw Ms. Romanello pretending to be watering her plants, but her attention was really focused on Wilbur and his surprise guests. Wilbur didn't have to speculate on the source of the complaint.

Officer Stern joined his partner, who was upchucking his double burrito dinner.

"Jumping Jesus! What are you running here, a slaughterhouse?"

With the lid off, the stench was nearly overwhelming. All the animal corpses combined with the smell of Officer Tacit's regurgitated burritos made a backed-up septic tank seem like the finest French perfume.

Stern, eyes watering, opened the closest garbage bag. "You sick bastard."

Wilbur tried to explain, while hearing his rights being read. It was all in the name of science. As he was being cuffed, the cat rubbed up against his ankle. Wilbur's struggles were misinterpreted as signs of resistance.

Officer Stern reacted with his mace.

Wilbur choked, his tongue tripping on syllables like a trapped mouse squirming for freedom. He needed his inhaler--some water at the very least. He had to make them understand what was at stake. His eyes burned like little ants were biting his pupils. He needed to rub them, but was constrained.

Squinting through blinding pain, he watched as the cat, tail swishing, grew smaller and smaller in the distance. Sounding like an electronic meow, the police siren echoed briefly, then grew silent; no need to alarm the neighbors.

MY GOTH
PROM DATE

The scream caught him off guard. Not that he wasn't used to bloodcurdling shrieks. His neighbor, Jurassica, cussed her boyfriend of the week on a regular basis, using language that would make Larry Flynt blush. He was use to it. This particular screech would have a death metal drummer plugging their ears. From such a beautiful throat too. He didn't think he looked that bad; there was only so much grooming one could do without a mirror. He had a mirror; Roland just didn't have a refection to call his own.

Unconsciously, Roland ran one hand pale as an albino's ghost through his hair. His post-death life could have been much worse. It's not like a vulture was perpetually pecking his kidneys or he was stuck making telemarketing calls for the Infernal Revenue Service. Roland was cursed, perpetually 19. At least he wasn't in need of a walker or diapers. Who wanted to be a vampire *and* an AARP member? His fake ID worked, too. Death had cured his acne. Now his money went towards instant tans and mouthwash. Roland had graveyard breath that made werewolf BO smell like overpriced French perfume.

"Oh my God! You look adorable."

The source of the compliment and shriek was Mitsy, his girlfriend. Dressed in black, she could have been the cover girl for an issue of *Funeral Times*. Stylish and scary. His eyes devoured her, stopping at her waistline.

"Is that new?"

"This?" petite hands showcased her chrome casket belt buckle. "Isn't it just to die for? I won it on *SCREAMbay*."

Mitsy loved dressing up. Tonight gave her an excuse. The Squaresville Community College they attended was having their annual dance for Continuing Ed students. Roland remembered the few high school dances he had previously attended. Talk about *Night of the Living Dead*. Even if he had a heartbeat, it would have failed to quicken at the opportunity to waltz around like a constipated corpse. Strip-searching a mummy would have been more fun. Reluctantly, he agreed to go.

Mitsy's lace skirt was dark as a bat's belly. Her stockings, fishnets with custom rips, revealed flawless skin. She wore Frankenstein boots, capable of crushing small rodents. Roland felt underdressed in his black suit and navy blue shirt but there was no way he was wearing a cape and red cravat as Mitsy suggested.

She hugged him, tight like a toe pincher coffin.

"Is that an inverted crucifix in your pocket, or are you just happy to see me?" she purred, batting lashes as long as spider legs.

"You look great too, Mitsy."

"You forked-tongue Romeo. You know where flattery will get you." She grasped his dark blue tie and gave him a loud smooch.

Roland knew. So far flattery had gotten him a smaller savings account. Girlfriends didn't come cheap. When he tried the old mesmerizing trick to save some coin, Mitsy said, "If you see something green, pick it off and shove it."

They had met at night school. Mitsy was studying taxidermy as a hobby and a way to make extra money apart from her day job as a vet tech. Roland pursued an Accounting degree. He knew the old saying about death and taxes, having experienced both. In his pre-death life, he was a pizza delivery driver. The job provided spending money during his freshman year in college. In fact, it was a customer who was short of cash but long of tooth and drunk on Lugosi-knew-what that converted him. Not that he had minded. Natalya was a Russian beauty queen, a runner up in the Miss Vladivostok pageant. He lost his virginity that night too. Still had the scars.

It was the classic May-December romance and doomed from the start. Natalya was over 300 years old, (but didn't look a day over 40) but didn't have the patience to take someone under her wing, so to speak. His Russian Winter over, Roland tried returning to his previous life but his skin's tendency to deep fry in sunshine made attending day classes impossible.

Roland made an attempt at what he thought was the vampire lifestyle, He frequented Goth clubs and horror conventions but realized while he wasn't exactly aging, he wasn't getting any younger either. Roland decided on a more practical future and resumed his education.

While undergoing the torture known as class registration, Mitsy, in line behind him, asked Roland about his complexion, did he have a disease or was he just naturally pale? She was jealous either way. Roland said, "A little of both."

Their first date was a midnight screening of *Bride of Re-Animator*. Roland didn't get it. It wasn't scary. An audit. That was scary. Afterwards they shared pizza at No Anchovies. Between slices, they learned they shared a hatred of onions and a morbid fear of Siamese twins. Mitsy was smitten with his arched eyebrows and he was drawn to her pulse.

"I have something for you," Roland said.

With a pickpocket's grace, he presented Mitsy her corsage. Roland fumbled between lace and breast, piercing his thumb.

"Better let me do that. That's the wrong kind of prick," she said with a wink.

Thumb in mouth, Roland refrained from comment.

They piled into her Honda Civic. A psychedelic skull dangled from the rearview mirror. Inside, Roland was assaulted by what was surely the soundtrack to the Apocalypse.

"You'll dig this," Mitsy exclaimed, "It's a remix of Motley Crue's 'Shout at the Devil' done by the Electric Hellfire Club. It rocks."

Roland nodded his head, inwardly praying for an accident, anything to silence the speakers.

Mitsy drove like someone whose education behind the wheel stemmed entirely from playing video games, zeroing in on possible obstacles and jerking her stick shift like it was sexual fetish. Her eyes neither moved nor blinked. Roland, his nerves already taunt from the skull shattering music, closed his eyes and silently chanted, "I will survive.'

Miraculously, they arrived at the college. The lot was already overcrowded. Roland, anxious to feel the Earth beneath him, pointed to an open space. Mitsy acqui-esced; normally she refused to pay for parking, content to drive in spirals until a spot miraculously appeared.

The gymnasium decorations could best be described as "what the budget would allow" with a bit of "yard sale" flair. Balloons moved like demented strands of mutant DNA. No live band, just a DJ. Roland thought it sounded like Tina Turner's "It's Only Love." The last time he had heard the song seemed like a lifetime ago.

It was a sizable turnout. People of various ages, bra sizes and hairlines out to have a good time. It was a great way to blow off steam before midterms.

"This music sucks. Let's look for drinks."

Like a werewolf pup following the arc of the moon, Roland trailed after Mitsy.

"Stand here. Pretend you're a Medusa suitor."

Roland stammered, "What?"

"Stand still, stud."

Mitsy reached into her bag, rummaging around like a magician in search of a stray bunny. Presto. She produced a flask.

"Vodka," she said in a conspiratorial whisper. She offered to punch up Roland's punch. Roland declined, shaking his head like a possessed adolescent.

"Better make mine a double then."

Roland wished alcohol affected him. It's going to be long night, he thought to himself.

Something by Huey Lewis blared from the speakers. Roland nodded his head in time to the music. This was more like it. He hummed along to "If This Is It."

Mitsy finished her drink, wiped her mouth with her hand and yanked Roland towards the dance floor.

Several couples gyrated to the music. Mitsy didn't dance so much as she whirled, arms frenzied, like a traffic cop with palsy. Still, there was a certain style to her movements, convulsive as they might be. Roland wasn't one to criticize. Death had done nothing to loosen his inhibitions on the dance floor; he was as stiff as any occupant at the Squaresville morgue.

In mid Cabbage patch, a rather bony elbow caught Roland just below his left lung. With supernatural speed, Roland turned to face… a mime.

No, not a mime. Somewhere beneath all the makeup Roland smelled decay. The tux-encrusted zombie grimaced. So did Roland. Ugly didn't look good on the zombie, but it didn't appear to be leaving any time soon.

Roland tensed, preparing for the worst.

The zombie smiled, revealing teeth like yellow chalk.

"Sorry, dude. My bad." The voice sounded like an asthmatic with black lung.

Roland inwardly sighed. That could have been much worse. Zombies tended to run in gangs, the Crypts being the worst. You'd see them on the street just hanging out, guts on display, flashing their hand signs if they had the requisite number of fingers. Nothing sadder than an O.G. gone to rot. At one point just after being vamped, he'd considered joining the Bloodz but then thought about membership dues and reconsidered.

The zombie's date was no spring daffodil either. She was a Cemetery Mary all right, a real bone crone, a graveyard groupie of the first order. She had a cheerleader's body marred by the haggard look of a failed suicide or formaldehyde huffer. Still, if she played her tarot cards right, Roland thought, she might get her just dessert, no matter how spoiled.

Misty pressed her body against his. Tonight was his lucky night. He felt the excitement in her pulse, in her wrist, in her neck. He couldn't have been more jazzed if he was leaping tax brackets.

"I'm hot," Mitsy said, fanning her self. "I need some air. Let's go."

Roland, lost in the maelstrom that was Mitsy, headed for the exit. In the library parking lot, beneath a voyeur moon, Mitsy pulled Roland close.

This was it. His body tensed. The moment he had pantomimed through the dating rituals, listening to the soul-crushing stories of work and friends and family. Like he could give seven shades of hell about that stuff. This was it, the moment a virgin neck would be offered of her own free will. Roland wondered if he was drooling.

Mitsy looked up, eyes glistening. Neck, inches and inches of skin bared, blue hint of the jugular tempting and teasing, and oh so close.

"So … what do you think of . . ."

Her words, the one thing Roland hadn't, couldn't expect. It was like a sucker punch to the soulless, dispelling all myth and legend, all rhetoric and hyperbole and hype. Her words spoke truer than any wooden stake. Metamorphosis failed. Hypnosis failed. His unnatural defenses were tapped, all resources gone. Her words burned hotter than any sun. He couldn't blush but his skin felt like it had gone nova.

"So … what do you think of … marriage?" she asked with eyes all a twinkle.

Roland's life flashed before him. He didn't blink so much as wince.

The "M" word. Not monster or macabre, mutation, meningitis or Mephistopheles, not masochism, malaria or Marxism.

The "M" word.

Magic most black.

He gagged, no air available, his trachea turned tourniquet. His mouth transformed into a black hole, allowing not a single syllable to escape.

"Come on. Don't be such a stiff. I'm a serious. I don't plan on being single forever."

Without skipping a heartbeat, no pause for breath, Roland returned her stare and stuttered, "I think they are playing our song."

Ian Curtis' lyrics about love tearing you apart echoed

"It's not like I'm in a hurry. I'd want to live together first."

For the first time in his afterlife, Roland experienced a chill, like an ice cube enema.

"No pressure. Just stuff to think about. Hey, how cool is that DJ? Can you believe he's playing my Joy Division request?"

Roland looked towards the night sky for some sign or symbol. The full moon shrugged as clouds obscured the view. Mitsy pulled Roland's mouth to hers. Roland wondered what he was, bloodsucker or just a sucker for romance. Where would his coffin fit in Mitsy's apartment anyway?

DEVIL'S ADVOCATE

Dear Annie: I am 18 years old and getting ready to start my first year of college. My problem is my sister Wendy, who I love to death. Wendy recently became engaged to a guy named John. She asked me to be her bridesmaid. The problem is John and I have had sex twice, no, three times. The second time I was drunk. Does that count? The first time lasted about 30 seconds, which isn't really sex, is it? I wasn't even close to climax. The third time was just after the engagement announcement and was just goodbye sex and the best yet. I know now it was all a huge mistake, and I am really sorry it ever happened. Anyway, my question is, do I tell my sister about my encounters with John? I want her to have the best. John's a great guy, just not that good in bed, and I only want Wendy to be happy. I know if I tell her it will break her heart and she'll wind up hating me. What should I do?
--Torn in Toledo

Dear Torn In Toledo: Kill yourself. It's the only thing you can do. You have already shattered your sister's heart. Telling her would just be grinding the pieces. Haven't you caused enough pain? You can't be trusted. You have no integrity, no morals. You have no reason to live. Every breath you take is a lie. Guppies are a more evolved life form and are more loyal than you and they eat their young. Do yourself, your wounded sister and the world a favor and kill yourself. I suggest pills. It's not messy and you have caused enough pain and misery. Don't leave a note. You're not worth it.

Dear Annie: I am an 18-year-old female. I have been working at an office supply store to save money to attend beauty school in the fall. I get along with everyone except for my boss. He constantly stares at my breasts and makes rude comments. With help from a breast enhancement through hypnosis CD I purchased, I managed to go from an A cup to a full C but that doesn't give him or anyone else the right to ogle my new voluptuous chest. I find his eye to nipple discussions very disconcerting. How should I handle this? I really need the job.
--Fully Loaded

Dear Fully Loaded: If that son of a bitch is harassing you, he's probably doing the same to others. It's time to end his nonsense right now. I suggest a Hungarian Hi-Power .45 pistol. Available for less than 300 bucks with a fashionable wood grip and a four-inch barrel, making it easy to conceal, this baby should end your pervert problems. And when the jackbooted agents of the law show up, I suggest a TEC-9, available through your finer corner drug supplier. With that kind of firepower, those bastards with a badge won't have time to stare at your chest.

Dear Annie: I just wanted to say thanks. Your tips on dealing with that nosey priest were right on the money.

The holy water and second-rate exorcisms, while funny at first, quickly became annoying. The altar boy gimmick was particular effective. The last I heard, our "Father" had been defrocked and was sharing a cell with a former gang leader nicknamed "Trunk." The past does come back to haunt you, doesn't it?
--Hell Yeah

Dear Hell Yeah: Unwelcome houseguests can be amusing, but usually wear out their welcome faster than a would-be messiah. Let me hear you say "hallelujah." Glad I could be of infernal service.

Dear Annie is the penname for Anamalech. An expert on the human condition, Annie has been giving advice for years, usually for free. World leaders, movie stars and the movers and shakers of our time have paused to hear her words. Her books, Pain and Suffering and You, Strychnine for the Soul and Pull the Trigger are all best sellers. When Annie speaks, the world heeds her advice.

SHOP TILL YOU DROP

Screams wake Rose from her slumber. She sits up, disoriented, looks at the clock. 9 o'clock. Jumping Jesus. She overslept. The noise again, like a cheese grater on her ears. Not screams at all, just the neighbor's dogs. Shut up, she bellows. A hush falls over the neighborhood. The dogs, twin Dobermans with a taste for stray squirrels, cats and small fingers, now cowered, return to beneath the porch, tails tucked, eyes watchful for the source of the roar.

Rose yawns, no time to screw around. She's already late. Rose works as a housekeeping supervisor assistant at a local hospital. She rarely gets a Sunday off and aims to make the most of this one. She steps out of her cloths and into the shower in one smooth motion, the toothbrush in one hand, the other reaching for the soap.

The bathroom is still steamy by the time Rose is fully dressed, save for her shoes. She dashes to the kitchen, two slices of bread in the toaster and a tall glass of chocolate milk to wash it down. She's already wolfed down a banana before the toast is ready. Strawberry jam applied to the toast, she gives it a glance. Almost artistic. One bite and the masterpiece is half gone. Between mouthfuls, she retrieves the paper from the lawn, one eye watchful for disobedient hounds. Rose leafs through the paper, ignoring the boldfaced headlines proclaiming National Emergency. "Just some other reason to raise taxes," she reasons, annoyed. She bypasses the employment section, sports, business and the classifieds. She pulls out the TV listing for later perusal, then finally grasps her own personal Holy Grail, the ads. Rose devours the ads like a fat man at a Chinese buffet. Nothing escapes her notice. All 2-for-1 deals are filed in the folds of her brain. She scans the recesses of her memory for coupons already clipped. She is preparing for the forthcoming battle and she will not be denied. She finishes her milk, a chocolate mustache disappearing with one swipe of her forearm. My shoes, Rose thinks. Where are my shoes?

She emerges from the bedroom, purse in hand and fully sneakered. She yells goodbye to her husband Duane, already slouched in his chair in front of the TV, waiting for today's football games to begin. She's out the door before Duane can reply.

Rose squeezes into the rusty Toyota pickup. The truck groans. Rose is fat. She knows it. She doesn't need a scale; every movement reminds her. But she's used to it. As she grew into adulthood, her weight grew with her. The family doctor encourages exercise. Rose complies, walking to The Ice Cream Castle at least twice a week, six full blocks from her house. She rewards herself with a jumbo vanilla shake, forgoing the whipped cream; it gives her gas.

Her husband is no picture of health either, unless it's the typical "before" picture. Three hundred pounds if an ounce and most of it in his gut, Duane's only exercise today will be lumbering from his chair to the fridge, to refill on beer and snacks. If he's feeling really energetic, he'll waddle to the door for pizza, Chinese, Mexican or whatever nationality he's craving for delivery.

A news broadcast crackles from the dashboard speaker as Rose turns the ignition key.

"…that the dead may be..."

She twists the dial. Highway to Hell. Now, that's more like it.

"Nobody's gonna slow me down," she croons, tapping to the beat.

"Maybe I have time to stop for doughnuts," she thinks to herself. That might be cutting it a little close. She'll have at least an hour of driving ahead of her, traffic notwithstanding. "Damn churchgoers," mumbling to herself, "Why can't they worship in front of the TV. Like Duane." She snorts laughter at her own joke.

As she zooms past the doughnut shop exit, the nearly forgotten fragments of a dream derail her train of thought. Muffins. She had been dreaming about muffins: all types of muffins: blueberry muffins, chocolate muffins, muffins filled with fruits, spices, nuts and liqueurs. Their only commonality: They're all delicious.

But the muffins were chasing her, on tiny muffin legs. The muffins had teeth, much too large for their muffin bodies. She remembers kicking one; it bled cream. The pastries were fast. In her dream, she manages to barricade herself behind a door. The muffins whisper, "We won't hurt you. We're yummy. We think you're yummy too. Let us in and we can be yummy together." The muffins squeeze through the slit of the keyhole, through the cracks. They smell so good.

She doesn't remember the rest of the dream, thanks to those damn dogs. Just as well. Her stomach grumbles.

Minutes and miles pass in smooth cadence to Rose's thoughts, which ping pong between the fantasy of a soap opera hunk (who looks curiously like Dr. Rex up on the fifth floor), his stomach smooth and smelling like peppermints, and sweaty anticipation of the multitude of bargains that await. The intoxication of Red Tag stickers, clearance items and the all-important End-of-Summer sale sends her head reeling. She grips the wheel, knuckles cracking, and begins to hum. Restless, she spins the radio dial, finding mostly static. Finally, a voice, breaking, cracking, almost in tears, "… the end is here, brothers and sisters, the end is…" "The end is here… for you." Rose thinks to herself, smiling as she snaps the radio off, better to drive in silence than listen to that ear pollution.

She surveys the landscape, still hardly any traffic. A WGON news van speeds past her in the passing lane. Men armed with guns and beer cans form a single-file parade in a field; squirrels, rabbits, and street signs beware. Probably members of the National Guard playing soldier. Men and their war games. Off to the left is the meat-processing plant. Funny, for years it was just a slaughterhouse. Now with all the new development, it has a name change. Too bad they can't change the smell. Protestors usually gather outside the gates. They harass the passing motorists with signs, coupled with moronic, but energetic paroxysms of chanting, but today only their signs are present, leaning against the chain-link fence, useless like their owners. "Too lazy to even take their crap home," Rose muses to herself as she pulls at a stray strand of hair. "Either that or the plant is giving out free breakfast samples and the veg heads are all in line. 'Processed chicken parts equals genocide,' my ample ass. Wait till they find out tofu causes cancer and impotence. That will really give them something to protest." Rose winks at the reflection of herself in the mirror.

The mall dominates the horizon. Whoever invented shopping malls deserves to be on a stamp. Hell, maybe even their own national holiday. Rose takes a hard right, just clipping the curb. The truck wobbles. She has arrived, in nearly record time too. The Promised Land awaits.

"Everyone must still be sleeping; the lot is nearly empty, save for a dozen or so cars." Rose compliments herself for her foresight, brilliant planning and excellent driving ability allowing for her arrival at the stores before all the other malloholics show up.

Just after 10 a.m., she feels that she owns the place. Squeezing out of the truck (again groans), Rose walks the 30 yards to the glass-paneled doorway, panting after yard #15. She notices some teenagers squatting near the corner building. Hungover probably, she thinks. Dope fiends, strung out on that new drug. What was it? Oh yeah, Liquid Funeral. It sounds more like a perfume those emaciated Goth bitches would wear. WGON had a big expose all about it. In her day, cheap wine was all you needed to get high, not eating glue or snorting chemicals. Kids these days. Goddamn idiots.

Rose pushes on the metal bar and enters the shimmering cathedral of consumerism, greeted by soothing electronic music. It makes her feel like she's on hold. The plaza rings hollow in response to the sugary refrains, the only sound except the squeak of her tennis shoes upon the hard concrete floor.

She walks past the Eyeglass Shack, past Underwear Unlimited, past the Piercing Pagoda. Some of the stores had yet to open; their gates were still shuttered. The mall was unusually empty today; a few early risers, the usual assortment of geriatric mall walkers judging by their stumbling gait but none of the hardcore shoppers she usually encountered. Not that Rose was complaining. The playing field was wide open and Rose considers herself the home team.

Having already exceeded her normal exercise routine, which consisted mainly of household labor and unregimented snacking, Rose is still hungry. Burger City lay just around the corner. As she approaches, she notices a crowd formed just outside the entrance.

"Does the line start here?" she queries a haggard-looking gentleman standing near the end. Receiving no audible reply, she takes her place behind Mr. I-Forgot-to-Wash. Looking down, she notices the man's suit is slit down the backside, both the pants and jacket.

"Fashion." But looking at his shoes, what she took for grey socks is, in fact, pale, grey flesh. The hygiene of some people. She is hesitant, weighing her options: to stand in line behind this stinking homeless person, or to make tracks for the Doughnut Hole at the other end of the mall, when her decision is made for her. The bum slowly turns around, revealing a face that belongs in the grave. The rot and the stench are bad enough but this poor bastard must have been in some type of horrible industrial accident as part of his face is missing. Flies and other insects are having a picnic with the surviving scraps. What appeared to be a bone peeked through like an unexpected guest. The guy needs a closed casket funeral, not a cheeseburger with fries on the side. Better make that a formaldehyde shake with extra preservative. Supersize.

Rose turns to leave, sensing that Graveyard Face is surely getting ready to hit her up for change. She moves every bit as fast as her plus-sized figure would allow, avoiding the bum's grimy reach. The Doughnut Hole it is. An even dozen just to put that poor bastard's face out of her mind.

She passes the electronics store where most of the TV's are broadcasting snow, save one. That set, bargain-priced at $179.00, frames the face of the midday anchor at WGON. Rose thinks of her as Barbie Bitch because of her resemblance to the doll and her constant complaints. The regular news people must be on special assignment. Barbie rattles on something about "... every dead body that is not exterminated becomes one of them." Must be some type of new pest control problem. Rose notes to have Duane fumigate. She did not tolerate roaches.

Out of the corner of her eye, Rose sees two things. The first is that she has made a new friend as the bum from Burger City is shambling slowly towards her. The curse of having a friendly face and a Rubenesque figure. The other item, much higher on Rose's scale of importance, a table staffed by two small girls, girls in uniform. Light bulbs of recognition firework within Rose's head. Girl Scouts, and by implication, Girl Scout cookies. Rose loves Girl Scout Cookies. Thin Mints are a particular weakness. She beelines for the table, with Graveyard Face all but forgotten.

Rose steps to the table, summons a smile, when she is struck by the immediate realization that something is wrong. She forgot to stop at the bank; she doesn't have any cash with her. A check it will have to be. She digs into the abyss of her purse, extricating both her checkbook and a pen.

"Eight boxes of Thin Mints, please, and who should I make the check out to?"

The girls could do with some sun. Pale as chalk, Rose notes. They stare at her with empty, bored eyes. Rose, one eye on the girls, the other on the cookies, is taken completely off guard as the nearest girl lunges forward, sinking her teeth into Rose's checkbook. What the hell? The other girl grabs at Rose's free hand but Rose is used to the pleading clasp of hospital invalids. She avoids the girl and jiggles backward when her movement is halted. She spins, her nostrils recognizing her barrier before her eyes. Graveyard Face is back. This time Rose has no time for politeness. She's been at the mall for approximately 20 minutes and has yet to purchase anything.

Rose drops her purse from the crook of her arm into her hand. Given its contents of various bottles of perfume, a hammer in case of emergency, candies of various sizes and tastes, and just under 11 bucks in small change, the purse is a most formidable accessory. Much like Mjölnir, the fabled hammer of Thor, the Norse God of Thunder, only those deemed worthy are capable of hefting Rose's purse. Assuming the coiled stance of a major league hitter pursuing a homerun, Rose smacks Graveyard Face right in the not-so-sweet spot. Bugs and flesh fly. Rose winds up on the advancing scouts, smashing each in turn, lawsuits be damned. The girls drop like rocks. A double for the home team.

All this commotion gathers a crowd. Rose suddenly realizes the mall walkers have worse problems than arthritis or weak bladders. It's like a Leper convention, grinning skulls, jigsaw puzzles of skin, faces as green as a black-and-white film re-colored. It's a veritable pukefest.

Rose straight-arms the nearest shopper, acquiring momentum, as she zigzags through the festering crowd. Rose bulldozes through them like a fullback with diarrhea headed for the nearest bathroom. They rise unblinking and unfeeling, like store mannequins. She clotheslines a security guard, his face already rouged with rot, knocking both his shoes and feet off. Rose is too busy to notice. Fuck shopping; she just wants out of here and perhaps some dessert.

Outside the mall, she finally reaches her car and is confronted by a trio of Gucci girls turned ghastly. Either due to some buried primal group memory or just out of habit, the girls giggle at the fat woman fumbling with her keys. Sounding like someone with throat cancer or choking on wet bread, the girls continue to hack and titter, giving Rose ample time to secure herself into the driver's seat. She forces the pickup into gear. When the irresistible force (Rose's truck) meets the rotting object (Gucci girls), the result equals splat. The girls, no longer slaves to fashion, makeup or popular opinion, only diet, writhe on the pavement like spiders with limbs removed.

She wheels past a security guard, who curiously resembles Keith Richards. The truck backfires putting an exclamation point to her thoughts.

"What the fuck was that all about?!"

The needle burns on 65 all the way home, the highest speed the Toyota will allow before having convulsions.

She arrives in the driveway just as a pizza delivery driver pulls up two doors down. Dumbfounded, she watches as the driver plows into the front of a Volkswagen Bus. Boy, those hippies are going to be pissed. The driver gets out the car, one hand holding the pizza like some underpaid Statue of Liberty. The other hand still grips the steering wheel. The driver looks at Rose, motions to wave but seems to realize he's missing a key ingredient in the gesturing process.

Rose opens the door. Home, sweet home. Duane manages a grumble. She plops on the couch. She stares at her husband, already three days dead, slowly becoming one with his chair. Rose grabs the remote from his swollen hand.

"And give me some of those chips, too."

Rose makes herself comfortable, realizing the more things change, the more they stay the same.

Outside, the dogs and delivery driver eyeball each other. Guess who's dinner?

HOLLYWEIRD AND VINE

Her skin was as dark as licorice and just as sweet. She had spit that line more times than she could count on fingers manicured by West Hollywood's more fashionable nail techs. The line worked. All part of the advertising. If there was one thing Dorthea could do, it was sell, her favorite product being herself. She had the face of the girl next door, if the girl had grown up in Chicago slums, traded the urban decay of the Midwest for Tinseltown dreams at the age of 17 and spent the next eight years living and learning on the street, on her back and on her knees, in alleyways and back seats, front seats and the occasional hood. If things worked out as she hoped, she would be retired from the game before the game could retire her, like it had so many other girls in her profession.

At 5'8 and 134 lbs, she wasn't a statuesque beauty but Dorthea could definitely handle her shit, putting the hell in bombshell when she was pissed. She had left her mark on more than one overly aggressive customer. She had learned the hard way; every scar was a lesson, an A+ on the Survival report card. Her body was lean but not without curves, like coiled and oiled steel, although years of living on the outskirts of life had faded the shine.

Dorthea might have been born at night, but it sure as hell wasn't last night. She thought she'd seen it all on this corner. But this was a new one. The john in the Honda waved at her, like an epileptic on a sugar high.

"Hey whore, Big Daddy wants to party."

A class act, this one.

Big Daddy had a wad of cash the size of a double Monster Burger, unfortunately it was Monopoly money, currency the color of childhood. Poor fool, thinking he could pull a fast one. He probably would be a fast one, too, thought Dorthea. He must have left his common sense in his other pants.

He probably had a Get-Out-of-Jail-Free card stashed in his wallet in case of emergency.

Good luck with that one, Big Daddy, she thought. Play that orange card on the hometown fuzz and their batons would fall faster and hit harder than the Reading Railroad and land with greater frequency. Dorthea knew that as gospel. So did the world. It had been televised time and time again. LA cops might not know how to shoot straight but they were pretty handy at welding a big stick. Clubbing 101 must have been a prerequisite at the Academy.

"Come on, baby. Those lips look like they could suck the red out of a clown's nose. I ain't got all fuckin' day."

Dorthea reached down into her cleavage and pulled out a badge. She told Big Daddy to make like a reject from a zombie movie and play dead.

His listening skills on par with his pick-up lines, Big Daddy put the pedal to the metal, just avoiding being T-Boned by a black BMW and took his party elsewhere.

Dorthea put the novelty badge she had gotten from a gumball machine back in her bra. Close up, any moron could see it was a toy but from a distance, not so much.

She hoped Big Daddy with his porn-star goatee and funny money didn't kill anyone in his search for a blowjob, handjob, rimjob or whatever particular party he was looking for. It's not like hookers were an endangered species in Hollywood. Working girls were only outnumbered by the cockroaches and that's because the bugs didn't use birth control.

Dorthea leaned against the streetlight. She thought of the streetlights as steel angels, straight and tall. She felt protected by the halo their light provided. In her world, protection was gospel, as important as condoms, fuck-me pumps, fishnet stockings or the free clinic.

Anyone working the streets could use all the help they could get, be it from the rare kind-hearted cop, a concerned social worker or a pimp who knew damaged goods cut into his cash flow. Everybody needed a second set of eyes. Dorthea included. She was already at a disadvantage; her left eye was gone, sacrificed to the street long ago.

Her one good eye scanned the area, imagining what it must have been like in the '20s and '30s when a concentration of radio- and movie-related businesses made their homes here. It was a far cry from what it was today: bums, winos and the homeless owned these streets now and their claim was greater than the names imbedded in the sidewalk. The Hollywood Walk of Fame still attracted the tourists, but there was something repellent about seeing your favorite celebrity's name right next to a pile of fresh human feces.

Everyone was a critic.

Sure, there were various projects attempting to restore the area its lost luster. Good luck with that one, thought Dorthea. It was a ploy by politicians to garner votes, millions of dollars worth of votes. The simple truth was you could renovate buildings but how did you fix the human spirit? What's the price tag on that?

Dorthea could tell you about hard times, explain the delicacy of a toothpaste sandwich when there was nothing else to eat, watching steam rise from your shit because it was so cold and there was no heat. Dorthea knew about hard times. She had paid her dues, gone from a ten-dollar blowjob queen to a credit card call girl, six stories below the penthouse. Some of her regulars required special demands. In her line of work, special meant you better have the cash to cover.

Boots was one of her regulars, one of her first legit customers, back when she had a genuine pimp calling the shots and not some boyfriend just playing the part. Merlin Jones was the pimp's name. A former stage magician turned flesh merchant. He was ancient when she met him (God rest his soul). He had eyebrows as thick as agitated caterpillars and a heart of gold. He was old Hollywood and had connections dating back to the silent era. She wasn't sure of his exact age but she could see dust when he spoke, always in whispers. He was a class act, even if it was an act. Vaudeville was in his DNA. Merlin had saved her life. She cried for days when he died, a victim of celebrity.

Merlin's pimp mobile, a '66 Toronado restored, was sandwiched between the latest tabloid queen and an overzealous shutterbug, rushing to capture the next front page. Merlin was the one who wound up squished, flatter than a June bug on a SUV windshield. The resulting wrongful death lawsuit and Merlin's will moved Dorthea from an apartment spitting distance from the sidewalk to the presidential suite.

In this town, publicity, good or bad, came with a price.

Boots was old Hollywood too, back when silver screen stars were just shades of gray. She called him Boots because of his choice of footwear, always those big black clodhoppers. Boots looked like a kink freak, as if the neck piercings and ritual scarification wasn't a dead giveaway. He favored wearing leather and studs, like he belonged backstage as a roadie for some death metal band or working as an S&M model. He was a misfit of science, masquerading as a man.

Dorthea liked Boots. He wasn't a talker like some; he was a man of action. A real man of the world, despite his limited vocabulary. Not well schooled, but certainly educated, he had given Dorthea an anatomy lesson she wouldn't forget on more than one occasion.

He was the only john that requested Dorthea leave her eye patch off. He thought it made her look like a pirate. Despite his appearance, Boots wasn't big on role-play and the only booty he was after was hers.

Boots had a fondness for toys, all sorts of buzzers and prods and things that went ZAP. He was gonzo for gadgets, like a seven-foot tall kid on Christmas morning. Truth be told, Dorthea almost preferred the artificial cocks. Boots own prick was so big it needed its own zip code.

Like nearly everyone else in Hollywood who had their cosmetic surgeon on speed dial, Boots had gotten some work done. He liked it when she stroked his stitching, among other things. Dorthea guessed (she dare not ask in fear of embarrassment, his, not hers) that he had even had some work done *down there*. Sometimes it was a different color. It could become erect in seconds, almost like he pushed an "on" button. It was like the damn thing had hydraulics.

Boots was the biggest guy she'd ever been with, either vertical or horizontal. His dates had to be scheduled well in advance, so she could stock up on lube, Goliath condoms, and plan days for rest and recovery. He left her sore and aching. He didn't mean to; it was just the nature of the beast.

He had the greenest eye she'd ever seen; the other one as blue as the California sky.

One good thing about Boots, he always paid cold, hard cash; the bills as green as his complexion.

Another of her regulars always insisted on taking her to dinner on their "dates." D was a real aristocrat, almost snobbish in personality. He wore more makeup than she did and knew it. He joked he should start his own cosmetics line, "Color Me Dead," for the Goth crowd.

Mascara princess or not, D loved Italian food but professed an allergy to garlic; it caused him to break out in hives. With him it was always Chicken Scarpariello, Beef Carpaccio, Baked Ziti or Tagliata. How he loved his red sauce and definitely knew his wines.

At each restaurant, he knew the staff by name and had his own private table. He frequently liked to thank the chef personally for a wonderful meal but would occasionally whisper under his breath, "Not nearly as good as Mama Cneajna use to make."

Dorthea, of course, was dessert.

Where Boots hardly said anything, an occasional grunt or a groan, D wouldn't shut up; he was a talker, as smooth as any politician. If he hadn't been a customer, Dorthea could have almost succumbed to his sexy accent.

For all of his feigned European aristocracy, D was at heart, a lonely guy in need of companionship, someone to talk to. At one point, he had been on top of the world, but bad business deals, various addictions, jealous husbands and angry villagers had all taken their toll on his fame and his fortune. But he was fighter. He'd been knocked down, reputation skewed, heart impaled, but always bounced back. Dorthea admired the guy. He was someone she could confide in. He'd been around, seen it all and lived, more or less, to tell the tale.

Dorthea told him about her unexpected pregnancy. She was the mother to a child she had only briefly seen. The father, Billy of the kindest eyes and the sweetest smile, too scared of the responsibility, had joined the Army. That decision had gotten him killed in a foreign land. The child had been put up for adoption. Dorthea went to live with her grandmother at her mother's request. Dorthea's mom had her own issues to deal with, like sobriety. Her dad was just a stand-in in a few old photographs; the guy she would question her mom about, "Who's this dude?"

Unfortunately, Granny had died of a heart attack. With nowhere to go and not wanting the court to make that decision, Dorthea hopped the Greyhound and headed west, eventually landing in California. She knew she was pretty and hoped to get a job modeling. Instead, her story became a cliched movie of the week.

Enter Ace with his box office good looks. At 28, to Dorthea he seemed worldly, goal-oriented, and someone worth knowing. He was a struggling actor just waiting for his big break. He'd done some modeling and a few commercials, or so he claimed. What he really wanted was a gig on a daytime soap. He believed that would be a great way to build a fan base. Working as the night manager at a strip club was just a way to pay the bills. And the dope he sold on the side… it was just some weed, an ounce here, an ounce there and he just sold to friends. No big deal right?

God, he was smooth, as smooth as Jazz. He was just waiting for that one big break.

The break was Dorthea's nose.

By then, her modeling career moving as fast as a sloth in a 100-yard dash, Dorthea had gotten a job as a dancer at Club Fantasy, where Ace worked. Things seemed to be working out. She had moved in with Ace, just sharing the rent at first but soon sharing his bed. Ace fucked like he was playing lead guitar in a speed metal band, lots of energy at a manic pace. Not that she complained. Besides, Ace had contacts and said he was trying to set her up with a few photographer friends.

Three months into the relationship she discovered a condom in his jeans when doing his laundry. When she confronted him, he set her straight on a few things. It was a give and take world. In order to get anywhere, you had to be willing to sacrifice. It was just fucking; it didn't mean anything. He loved Dorthea. When Dorthea objected, Ace responded with his fist.

Dorthea, already smoking Ace's weed and experimenting with whatever else materialized from his pockets, spiraled down into a world of booze and drugs and false comfort. It seemed Ace had expanded his pot business to include coke, meth and pharmaceuticals.

Dorthea was on her way to fast becoming another Hollywood statistic. True to his word, Ace introduced her to his photographer friends who took more from her than just her picture. They stole whatever dignity she had left.

When she objected again, Ace broke two of her ribs.

The ribs healed slowly. She couldn't dance but she could still suck dick, thus contributing to the rent. Ace had few complaints.

The turning point came when the cable was turned off. By then, Ace was using as much dope as he was selling. When the TV failed to turn on to the Lakers' game, he went 5150, trashing what little furniture they had, kicking her still damaged ribs, hitting her so hard square in the face, he broke her orbital rim.

Ace threw her out. Somehow, crawling, she made her way into the street. Then a curtain call of darkness.

When she woke, she was in the hospital.

The doctors couldn't save the eye.

With nowhere to go, the street became her home. Another fallen star. She did what she had to.

Rule number one in the Roach handbook. Survival. By any means necessary.

Then one day, there's this skinny, black guy motioning her over. He was so old, skin like parchment. His wrinkles had wrinkles. She couldn't imagine this dude having the energy to breathe much less fuck.

"My name is Merlin, and I have a proposition for you."

Didn't they all?

Move to reel 2.

She told all this to D. Not all at once, but over time, several dates. D was a friend of Merlin's as were all of Dorthea's clients. Special gentlemen with special needs, all of them fallen stars.

D was a talker, but he also listened.

His career was currently, shall we say, under the radar, and had been for years. You wouldn't know it to look at him, in his Gucci sunglasses and always dressed to the nines in his tuxedo, ready for the red carpet, even if the suit was vintage fashion and smelled faintly of mothballs.

D was an old-school romantic at heart. He liked holding hands and kissing. Dates with him reminded her of old movies where the guy and girl made out in the back seat. That's all they ever did on their dates; lots of talking and necking and the occasion blowjob.

The only real drawback was the hickeys, but nothing a little ice or Aloe wouldn't cure.

Larry had set up tonight's appointment. Larry wasn't really a customer, just a guy she knew. Larry knew Merlin Jones (God rest his soul) and that's how they had been introduced. Larry was a struggling stand-up comic and had been struggling for as long as Dorthea knew him. He and Merlin use to open each other's act. They had stayed in touch, on and off, since Merlin's demise.

Dorthea thought Larry was actually a pretty funny guy although his jokes sucked.

"Two vampires walk into a bar.

The bartender asks what will you be having tonight?

One vampire says warm blood and the other says water.

The bartender asks 'Why don't you want blood tonight, sir?'

The vampire pulls out a tampon and replied 'I'm making tea.'"

Yuck, Yuck, Yuck.

Dorthea thought "yuck" was the word all right, but that was Larry: Lewd, crude and mostly housebroken.

To support himself, Larry worked a variety of jobs, including but not limited to house sitter, figure model, taxi driver, barber, private detective and assistant manager at Paws, a dog grooming salon (that lasted a week).

Currently, he worked part time as a security guard at the Erotic Museum located just a few steps West of Liberace's star on the Walk of Fame. He also tended bar at Howlers, a comedy club.

Larry was a hard-working, blue-collar lycanthrope as you could find. He had a gravedigger's work ethic and a witch doctor's charm. He had a homemade BBQ sauce recipe to die for and made a killer Silver Bullet.

Ingredients"

-½ oz Peppermint Schnapps

-½ oz chilled Vodka

Put Peppermint Schnapps in first and pour chilled vodka in second.

It will cloud up with a silvery color.

Down in one, feel the rush, howl at the moon.

Larry sometimes reminded Dorthea of Ace. But where Ace only cared about himself as time and experience had proven, Larry had a heart as big as all outdoors.

Larry had almost convinced Dorthea he was just one break away from stardom. He was currently one of the main subjects in a documentary on urban werewolves. Unfortunately, the film was stuck in studio hell. His last screen appearance was on the TV show *COPS*, an indecent exposure incident that Larry included as part of his act, not the actual exposure bit, just talking about the clip.

Larry, God bless him, put the fun in dysfunctional.

It was Larry who had told Dorthea of the old gypsy legend. She was skeptical at first. Little Green Men on saucer-shaped floats parading down Las Palmas, protesting immigration laws seemed more likely. But that was Larry for you. Where did he come up with this shit?

"I've been around, DoDo."

DoDo was his pet name for her. She hated it. He knew it.

The legend concerned an ancient object that granted the user one wish. The object, crafted in ancient Egypt, was a wedding gift of the Pharaoh Khufu to his bride Merityotes.

Khufu worshipped Ra, the sun god, and served as Ra's representative on Earth. Divine right and all that. Nut was the goddess of the sky, Merityotes her body double, if you will. Ra was believed to enter Nut's mouth after setting in the evening and travel through her body during the night to be reborn from her vagina each morning. Sort of a double penetration gig, but not really. Nut pulled double duty. She, according to Larry, was also goddess of the dead. The pharaoh entered her body after death, from which he would later be resurrected.

"Don't roll your eyebrows at me. That's what the legend says. I couldn't write material this good."

Larry told her an object was recently unearthed in the Hohle Fels Cave in Germany. The stone object was believed to date back to 2580 BC. The object was currently on tour and was at the Erotic Museum.

Larry was on a first-name basis with the owner of the exhibit.

"So what is it?" Dorthea questioned.

"It's, hmm…it's a dildo."

"Is this another joke? I don't get the punch line."

"No joke. I swear. Cross my heart and… well you know."

Larry arranged a meeting with Dorthea and the curator.

Mary, the exhibit's curator, looking fresh from the Mesozoic era and dressed in black Armani, greeted Dorthea, with all the warmth of a December day.

"So you have an interest in my… artifact?"

Well, duh.

Dorthea, always a straight shooter, cut through the bullshit like a bone saw on a cadaver.

Larry had already clued Dorthea in on the expected terms of agreement; Dorthea gets custody of the petrified penis for 24 hours, to be returned in perfect condition, in exchange for said item spelled out in the contract.

From her purse, Dorthea produced a photo of Ace. Damn if he wasn't beautiful, like a lionfish, full of poison. She had kept the picture as a reminder, a warning sign of when things seemed too good to be true.

Mary, like a film in freeze frame, slowly handed the object to Dorthea.

It looked like a cock crafted in a Ceramics class by a retard. About 7 inches in length, slightly above average, Dorthea was surprised at how smooth it was.

Mary wheezed, pointing out aside from its obvious functionality as a sexual aid, the object could also be used for knapping flints.

Dorthea had no idea what that meant and didn't care to ask. She placed the stone cock in her purse. Curiosity getting the best of her, she asked what Mary wanted with Ace's photo, no disrespect intended.

Mary answered, "My husband has been away for... a while, traveling abroad, in this world and the next. He—I should say we—are looking for a more permanent residence in this country. The land of opportunity, eh? Larry told us about Ace, and we feel he can aid my husband's, shall we say, transition into this country. Cut through the red tape. My husband has the patience of Anubis. I, however, do not. We are looking for a... physical address for the short term, and possibly longer."

Mary proceeded to eat the photograph of Ace, swallowed it without benefit of a *blingH2O* bottle of water. Dorthea left with the phallic object, wondering about the dietary habits of foreigners and old people.

Dorthea took a long look at Hollywood and Vine. A wave of nostalgia swept her, the pimps and pigs, the johns and rival corner conquerors clouded her memories. She thought of Boots and D and her other irregulars; she wouldn't miss it. That she was sure of.

Inside her apartment, Dorthea took a long, luxurious shower. Toweling dry, she pulled the object from her purse. She lit a few 100% soy candles and cuddled up with satin sheets. Marvin Gaye sang about sexual healing.

Comfortable, she anointed the polished phallus with the prescribed ingredients as detailed in the gypsy's rhyme.

Vampire blood, gargled, not drunk
Mix with Dead man's spunk
Add two hairs from a werewolf's groin
From loin to lip, lip to loin
Coupled with sacrifice and prayer
Now make a wish, if you dare.

She rocked the stone cock between her thighs, slowly.

So hard.

The cock.

The decision.

Thoughts of the past, present and future.

Orgasm approaching, Dorthea made her wish.

What she really wanted, more than anything for herself, for her daughter.

A second chance.

THE AUDITION

It was the type of night when anything could happen. Opportunity bloomed in the moonlight. It was especially abundant at the fairgrounds where lady luck was no stranger. It was a place of chance and metamorphosis, a sacred place. Strange alchemy slept in the soil, waiting to be awoken.

The trees surrounding the fairgrounds had begun to change. Their leaves had turned blood red, pumpkin orange and as yellow as cat eyes in the dark.

A chill lingered in the air. Even the fat lady trembled despite her layers of girth.

Adjacent to the fairgrounds was a field-turned-parking-lot. It was as empty as a graveyard after the Rapture, the cars having long gone home, their drivers' safe in their beds. Tire tracks remained like the footprints of some exotic herd of ancient beasts. Still, an echo of calliope music drifted on the wind like a ghost hunting for a home to haunt.

Past the topple-the-milk-bottle games and the goldfish toss, past the shooting galleries and the stuffed animal prizes, past the Scrambler, the Tilt-A-Whirl, the Ferris Wheel and the Funhouse, past the sickly sweet smells of cotton candy, elephant ears and other fried delights, past the tents advertising the world's biggest rat and the all other other-worldly attractions, there stood a tent, without sign or symbol or welcome mat. Still, it was not without visitors.

Inside, the auditions had begun.

The man at the center of attention had a pencil-thin mustache and wore three gold hoop earrings in each ear. A stud decorated his nose. His shirt was unbuttoned to the navel. He looked like an escapee from a pirate ship or, perhaps, a hairdresser with a taste for kink. The man slowly rolled up his sleeves, revealing smooth yet muscular forearms. He bowed to each of the judges and then lightly blew on the objects in his hands before setting them free. Silver glinted in the air briefly before descending.

The judges watched. Knives falling fast held their attention. In inexperienced hands, it was an accident in the making. Nerves, the late hour, and palm sweat were all factors that could cause a mistake and a mistake could cost a finger or two.

Fortunately for him, the juggler was no novice. He found his rhythm. Each arc became greater, the catch and release faster and faster. Now the showman was coming out. Behind the back. A knife balanced on his nose between throws. The blades were acrobats, each maneuver calculated to precision, and picking up speed with each rotation. The juggler smiled, grew more confidant. The knives were shooting stars and he controlled their trajectory. He thought the performance was going very well, his skills with the blades apparent.

Pity he was playing to an extremely tough crowd.

Shivers the Clown yawned. Jugglers were a dime a dozen. His personal favorite had been a guy named George, God rest his damned soul. George had been born blind due to retinopathy. As a kid, his nonfunctioning orbs had been removed, replaced by artificial ones. His parents, members of the upper crust, desired to hide their son's deformity and their shame, no matter the cost. They were willing to pay plenty. It's no wonder George ran away at 16, leaving his parents to their shame, but relieved their burden was finally gone.

That George managed to survive was a testament to his strength of character; he didn't have any, willing to lie, cheat and more. George was willing to do whatever it took to see another sunrise, so to speak. George owned several sets of eyes. They were like jewelry to him. Some collected earrings and some collected watches but George collected eyes. His mood determined what he wore on a given day. Green meant he was up to no good, purple said, "Do not fuck with me," and red indicated he was looking to shock the rubes. Red always meant trouble. How George could tell them apart was a mystery Shivers had been unable to resolve. George always popped in the baby blues when hitting a new town. He claimed no woman could resist. Judging from his panty collection, it was tough to argue. George liked to keep souvenirs.

One thing was certain; he never lost a staring contest.

Aside from the blindness, the gimmick that made George unforgettable was when he would juggle his false eyes. He would ever so slowly remove them from his sockets, taking his time, letting the audience squirm. He would grimace and groan and quote Mark 9:47, "And if thine eye offend thee, pluck it out: it is better for thee to enter into the kingdom of God with one eye, than having two eyes to be cast into hell fire."

He would plop the offending eye into his mouth, proclaiming to the audience, "It's impossible to cast a dirty look with an eye as clean as mine," then showcase it to the crowd almost like he was passing judgment on them. Many times, he was.

Always the showman, George placed an emphasis on letting one eye drop during each act. Without fail, the audience always screamed. He would then kick the wayward eye before stumbling off the stage in hot pursuit.

He was fond of saying, "Better to be blind and have vision, than to see and have none."

George had a good attitude about his handicap. Of course, neither his attitude nor philosophy helped him when, coming out of a bar, fully fermented, he walked in front of a garbage truck. The impact knocked both eyes out of his skull, bouncing on the asphalt like runaway ping-pong balls.

A pity really, the clown thought. George was talent. A son of a bitch, but a talented son of a bitch. This guy was a snoozer by comparison.

Shivers produced a yellow balloon from one of his many pockets. He twisted and turned and contorted the balloon until it looked like a hydrocephalic infant. From a rainbow-colored stocking, he slowly withdrew a switchblade and proceeded to lobotomize the balloon child, producing a loud POP.

The sudden noise caused the juggler to miscalculate his catch. The knife, a cold, unforgiving mistress, bit deep into his index finger. The other knives fell like wounded birds. Blood spurted from the wound.

The clown chuckled like a crazed chimpanzee. The middle judge turned to his white-faced companion, mouthed the word "Asshole," and rose from his chair.

Dressed in a green suit and matching Fedora, Mr. Soot, the carnival's manager, resident czar of the bizarre and reigning wizard of odd, or so his business card read, helped the juggler gather his scattered cutlery.

The cut was a nasty one. Soot explained that while the juggler showed extraordinary dexterity and remarkable timing, he really needed to work on his focus.

Working birthday parties and Bar Mitzvahs was one thing; performing as part of the Carnival Pandemonium was a different kind of beast, requiring a special kind of performer. One didn't become part of the show based on talent alone. Unfortunately, the juggler failed the test.

Hermes Soot explained all this in soothing tones. He was of Asian descent but his accent was practiced Kentucky Pentecostal. As cool as a copperhead, Soot sounded like a doctor telling a patient they had terminal cancer or advanced emphysema. He said it with such warmth and sincerity the juggler forgot he was bleeding. It was the showman in him. He could sell condoms to nuns and damnation to the devout, but his true avocation had always been to entertain. From snake handling to magic tricks, it was ingrained in his DNA; it was in his blood. And sometimes, in the blood of others.

He escorted the poor dripping fool to the show's medic, a former veterinarian turned hog trainer. Pretty Patty and her Precocious Pigs.

He offered parting words of praise and encouragement, shook the juggler's non-knife-bitten hand, and thanked him one last time for his performance, apologizing profusely for the accident. Soot said it was a small wound and expected the juggler to be tossing knives again in no time.

Soot, his eyes as bright as mating fireflies said, "A true artist would be inspired by this night's events."

His words were syrupy enough to cover pancakes but he meant every one of them.

Mr. Soot returned to the audition tent. He had served as the Carnival's manager longer than he could remember and his memory was considerable. He had, in fact, hired his fellow judges, Shivers and Dr. Sawbones. Neither were virgins to the business of show business themselves.

Shivers was the youngest, both in terms of age and experience, but possessed a desire to make people laugh until it hurt that made Soot envious. He was a bald, black man decorated in white pancake make up. Black, jagged thunderbolts converged over his shaved eyebrows, ending on plump cheeks. His shirt was a collision of color, like ketchup, mustard and other condiments had chosen it as their battlefield. His pants were a mismatched checkerboard pattern and in need of a wash. His painted on sickle of a smile could reap laughter from the crowd, young and old alike.

Sawbones was the dinosaur and a consummate professional. He was as pale as Shiver's makeup, as thin as borrowed time, and civilizations collapsed between his sighs. As the show's human pincushion, he suffered for his art figuratively. His Bible was pain and it was writ on his skin as Scripture to be read daily. Every scar was testimony and each wound evidence of his love for his craft. "The show must go on," was his mantra, no matter the cost. Sacrifice was his middle name.

Soot was growing tired. In every town, they held open auditions, always hoping to find undiscovered talent. Some were summoned by invitation, by recommendation or by heeding some unexplainable internal call. The freaks and the geeks, the true outsiders, the rail riders, the mid-nighters, the tarnished and tainted, the losers and the lost, all migrated to the Carnival's call.

Thus far, the night's candidates had included:

A 300-lb stripper, dancing to Patsy Cline's "Pick Me Up On Your Way Down." Pass

Various pyromancers and self-immolation amateurs. Pass.

A pair of kickboxing midgets. They were hired after the first round.

An obviously skilled practitioner of origami, specializing in gross sexual anatomy and unorthodox bedroom positions. A definite possibility for the gift shop, if nothing else.

The Human Chopping Block. Pass.

The Human Etch-A-Sketch. Hired.

Various sword swallowers, glass walkers, razor blade eaters and a sole light bulb defecator. Pass.

A goldfish geek. Save it for the frat parties. Pass.

The Beekeeper. The performer smeared honey over her body and was then swarmed by bees. Very sensual but there were bestiality laws to consider, plus Soot was sensitive to bee stings and irate husbands (she was married). Pass.

The Human Mouse Trap. Pass.

The Freak. Wearing a cowboy hat, he introduced himself as Stu from Charlotte, NC. He unbuttoned his shirt, revealing another set of hands, perfectly normal, extending from slightly above his ribcage. Stu produced a flashlight from his back pocket and preceded to entertain the judges with the best shadow puppet show they had ever witnessed. Hired.

The Twins. They performed famous duets while fused at the lower chest. Under consideration.

After resuming his seat and telling Shivers, "No more funny business," Soot called in the final act.

Soot thought the performer belonged in a high-school yearbook, beneath the caption, "Most likely to be forgotten." He was young, dressed in dirty khakis and an ill-fitted tie. He looked like he needed a shower, a shave and a hug.

He introduced himself as Johnny Prester and mumbled, "I know things."

Shivers, cackling like a grandmother suffering dementia, asked, "Where is author H.P. Lovecraft buried?"

Johnny paused a second, an eternity, then answered "Swan Point Cemetery."

The clown's smile inverted, faster than an erection at an Eskimo brothel.

Dr. Sawbones wheezed, "That might win you some bar bets, but trivia's not gonna cut it here. What else you got, son?"

Johnny walked to where Dr. Sawbones was seated and extended a slightly trembling hand.

Sawbones had eyes the color of crow feathers, black as a buzzard's wing. He was ugly, like the bastard love child of Keith Richards and Abe Lincoln.

Johnny gripped Sawbones' hand, like grabbing a high-voltage electric eel.

Johnny, eyes egg-white, grimaced and said, "You are a Capricorn, the goat torn between the heights and the abyss. You are the return and the departure from the ever-spinning wheel of rebirth. You are the broken sword. You are Ahasuerus, cursed to forever wander."

The electric lights in the tent flickered.

Johnny continued, "You will be shot, burnt alive and run over by a hearse with flames graffitied on the fenders. You will be decapitated by a one-armed man. You will hang by your neck but will refuse to succumb to the Reaper's caress. You will not rest. No cemetery will have you. This is your future; this is your life."

Johnny released Sawbones' hand.

Sawbones blinked but otherwise remained as stoic as the embalmed.

Johnny wiped his forehead with his tie and rubbed his eyes, then moved to the clown.

With a gargoyle's grin, Shivers said, "I never wash after flushing. It's a phobia. Did you know that?"

Johnny grabbed the clown's hand.

Shivers shivered.

"You are Bielbog and Chernobog, day and night, the sun and shade. You are Gemini. You are Ouroborus, always devouring. Six is your number. You have a brother, Stitches, now dead. Shivers and Stitches. Comedy and tragedy. Mirth and Murder."

The clown struggled to get away but Johnny's hand was a vice.

Soot smiled, enjoying the show.

"I see twin torches, one ablaze and the other extinguished. You are Cain and Abel, the two-in-one. When you walk, you feel your brother's shadow. Stitches does not rest peacefully. He haunts you and delights in your sleepless nights. The Wheel of Transformation continues to spin. He waits for revenge."

Shivers was speechless, as were the other judges.

Soot continued smiling, allowing Johnny to compose himself. The young man shook like an addict in need of a fix.

"Pretty good show so far. I guess I'm next. Hot damn."

Soot extended both hands. The backs of his hands were adorned with tattoos of a bird and a fish. Johnny hesitated when Soot grabbed his hands.

"Good luck."

The clench was made.

Soot felt like he was dreaming. In the dream, he was on a spider's web. He felt vibrations on the web, indicating movement. He wasn't concerned; he knew he was the spider, not some luckless fly. The vibrations spoke to him.

"You are a Libra. You are the shepherd. The mirror without reflection, the skeleton at the feast. Your number is 11. You are the double spiral, the serpent within the spin, the coiled snake.

"You have no future."

Johnny quickly released Soot's hand.

Soot stared into the boy's bloodshot eyes.

"You don't say. That was a pretty piece of poetry, sheer music to my ears, prettier than a bird's song."

"What do you think, boys? I think we've got a winner. But first…"

From thin air, cards appeared in Soot's hands. The Tarot.

"Do me the honor and pick a card. Of course some say, the card picks you," he said with a wink.

Soot fanned the cards and Johnny picked one.

"Good choice!"

The card depicted two nude figures holding hands. One figure's head was that of a crescent moon; the other wore the face of the sun. Encircling their waist was a serpent. Above the figures was a cherub armed with a shotgun.

"You've lived a tough life, boy. I can see that, and I'm not even psychic. This gift of yours… it's something else. It's a powerful, dangerous thing. No one should have to bear your burden. The Carnival takes care of our own. Always has. Trust me on that."

Shivers began to applaud.

Dr. Sawbones cleared his throat, like the sound of sandpaper.

Soot put his hands on Johnny's shoulders.

"Welcome."

And they all lived happily ever after.

Shivers become a popular children's TV host, winning five Emmys in a row before retiring from showbiz to start his own foundation to aid orphaned children. His face adorned everything from coloring books to underwear.

Dr. Sawbones was declared a medical marvel. He proved to be the perfect guinea pig and tests on his unique physiology led to several important medical breakthroughs in battling disease.

Hermes Soot stayed with the Carnival until it eventually went bankrupt. He then disappeared. It was rumored he became a monk, tending to lepers.

Johnny Prester became a pundit, frequently appearing on television news shows and was the author of several books, including the popular series "Tomorrow's Headlines Today."

At least, those were possible futures, events that, had the stars allowed, could have come to pass. But it was a night when anything could happen.

And this was what did.

Soot ruffled Johnny's hair.

Tears fell from the boy's face.

Soot reached into his jacket's pocket and pulled out a pack of cigarettes and offered Johnny one.

Johnny silently declined.

Soot took the cigarette, stuck the lit end in his mouth, breathed deeply, and expelled a fireball directly into Johnny's face.

Johnny was engulfed in flames. He screamed and batted his face to no avail.

Soot embraced the boy, pinning his arms as the flames burned a cobalt blue.

Johnny slumped in Soot's arms.

Soot held the body gently, smothered the flames with his hands, and addressed his fellow judges.

"Guess he didn't see that coming, huh? He was a little too good. No one should have that type of burden.

You could see it on his face; his life was a constant suicide he had to relive every day and would continue forever. No one needs that kind of pain."

Soot stroked Johnny's hair.

"I know."

Shivers and Sawbones relived Soot of his burden.

The auditions were over. Shiver's and Sawbones exited the tent.

Soot extinguished the light. His eyes glowed.

Outside, a flock of birds flew past the descending moon. The night was no longer quite as young but still the feeling was there—anything could happen, but diminishing now like a dream dissolved by daylight.

Soot, eyes full of hope but a heart of despair (or was it the reverse?), adjusted his hat and scratched his scalp. The Dragon Man smiled.

Pretty Patty's Precocious Pigs were in for a treat.

BUNNIES

Ant loved the bunnies. They felt good in his arms, soft and warm; they were bundles of furry goodness. He smothered them with gentle caresses. Sometimes they squirmed like wiggle worms to get away but Ant held them tight until they settled down, their movements compacted, restricted like canned sardines. Pops did not approve. Sometimes Pops smacked Ant in the head with his fist, each knuckle an exclamation point, and yelled the nastiest things, things that hurt Ant far more than the physical blows, and made him hide his eyes so Pops wouldn't see him cry. Ant witnessed his father holding the bunnies himself. He didn't understand why he wasn't allowed to do the same. Ant was never as rough as his father, never abusive. He used "kid gloves" as his father would say but never actually wore anything on his hands. He meant no harm. Ant wasn't a little boy anymore; he was a "big boy." Ant's father had to look up to meet his eyes. Ant did his chores without anyone telling him. He knew how to handle the bunnies. He spoke softly to them, relaxed them with his whispers. His father never, ever did that.

Pops looked like a porn star back in the days when the tits were real but the acting fake. He had a mustache that would have made Yosemite Sam jealous and was higher up the intelligence scale than most. He had the wallpaper to prove it. Multiple degrees no more useful than toilet paper. But for all his smarts, his parenting skills were little more advanced than the crocodile; he hadn't eaten his offspring. Yet.

Ant didn't like it when his father held the bunnies. He cringed when he touched them. When Pops touched them, they tried to get away. That made Ant's father crazy. Scary crazy. And the noises the bunnies made caused Ant to hold his ears. He plugged his thumbs in them as far as they could go, attempting to block out the sounds. He hated that noise and hated Pops, wished he would stop. Ant knew his father knew his actions were wrong and what made it even worse: Pops didn't seem to care. He always said it was "for the greater good."

The bunnies lived outside in a cage, behind their house, an old two-story lodge in the middle of nowhere that once served as a destination spot for hunters with big guns and bigger bank accounts. The Old Man and Pops had been paying guests a lifetime ago. The lodge had its own landing strip, long since reclaimed by weeds. Ant couldn't remember the last time he saw a plane.

The preserve once housed living targets of all kinds. Trophy boars, wildebeest, blackbuck antelope, watusi bulls, scimitar-horned oryx, Corsican rams, whitetail deer, among other species, roamed the hundreds of acres of hardwoods, planted pines, prime pastures and deep, dark swamps scattered throughout the preserve.

Now all that were left were the bunnies and they were not natives; they had been transplanted special. The cage that housed them was roofed but suffered leaks, especially during storms. During the spring and summer, it stormed a lot, like the clouds were going hunting, armed with lightning bolts and what they couldn't electrocute they intended to drown. Ant's father's father had built the cage himself years ago.

Pops and the Old Man constantly argued. The Old Man called Ant by his given name—Antonio—and called his son "Einsteiner" when he was in a mood, which was frequent, and would rag him about where his high-and-mighty thinking and advanced hocus-pocus had landed humanity.

"You poked holes in the land and the sea and the air and even in other damned dimensions with your scientific quests and when it came time to plug the holes, you think-tank boys were a little too late in the idea department. It was a matter of when, not if, something poked back. Mankind was damn near castrated in the process."

"Dad, I've told you an infinite amount of times, I had nothing to do with those projects. They were so hush-hush, I'm not sure anyone knows where the true finger pointing should have been directed. It was a lot of guesswork and denial. Anyone who had a smidgen of the truth is probably long dead. Remember the riots? People learned to vote with a bullet and they weren't too particular of the party or platform; they just needed a bulls eye. My field has always been engineering, mapping mankind's evolution, not digging graves. I'm a flashlight towards the future."

"Too bad your damn batteries are dead. You wouldn't know true north from an eagle's asshole and I've told you an infinity and one times, don't back talk me. There's only one hole you need to plug and that's the one between your nose and your dick and I don't mean your belly button so plug it.

"And what are you giggling about, Antonio? You don't have anything to laugh about. I've seen carp smarter than you. If you weren't blood, I'd done choked and smoked both your sorry asses by now."

The Old Man was bald but had eyebrows that looked like frightened caterpillars. A scar road mapped one side of his face, a reminder that the golden rule was bloodstained these days. Once upon a time, he had made the mistake of trying to convince a church full of believers that God wasn't the answer. Prayer was about as useful as a boot full of piss. Salvation meant moving their asses now before a bigger flock of Old Testament fanatics arrived to show them the error of their ways. "Love thy neighbor" didn't cut it; human sacrifice was the Word and the Way. The Old Man's pleas fell on deaf ears. The scar was their way of saying "No thanks, heathen." It wasn't the Mark of Cain, but he had learned his lesson. The Lord could help fuck-all; the Old Man looked after his own. He didn't expect a happy ending, but that didn't mean he wasn't going to try.

The Old Man scared the shit out of Ant with his outlandish tales of people who ate their own limbs, amputee societies that had flesh buffets courtesy of monthly meat lotteries or when they were lucky, unsuspecting travelers. He rattled on about legends of metal-armored demons piloting helicopters from Hell, raining bullets of brimstone on both the sinner and the sinless. His favorite stories involved scientists who had conjured horrors in secret government labs in hopes of feeding the starving populace and instead succeeded in breeding food that ate the stupid, slow and foolish and anything else their twisted vines and carrot teeth could reach.

The Old Man claimed to have seen firsthand a pumpkin patch, pumpkins the size of Volkswagens that had munched and mauled an entire mobile home community back when he was part of the Guard.

He would always give Pops the eye when he told that story, and Pops would just shake his head, more in frustration than denial.

The Old Man had died summers ago, his ashes scattered, and neither of his descendants missed him. Pops said his meanness killed him, but Ant figured it was more likely the homemade liquor. Even the smell of it caused Ant's eyes to water. The Old Man had been a bear of a man, all claws and growls, not quite as civilized. Ant had inherited his size and strength from him according to Pops.

The Old Man was as crazy as an ape on acid, but he was also a survivor. He could rig shit with a Kleenex, spit and old-fashioned American ingenuity, and if gunpowder was involved you could bet your ass something was getting blown to smithereens.

The cage was a mix of chicken wire, concrete blocks, spare automobile parts, 2 x 4's, a salvaged lion's cage, plywood and whatever else the Old Man cobbled from the remnants of the lodge and surrounding area. It wouldn't pass any builder's code but the damned thing worked, kept some things in and other things out. Parts of the cage were rusty but Pops wasn't concerned.

"I dare 'em to get away," he said with a smile. Ant was allowed to feed the bunnies. That made him happy. One of his chores was cleaning the cage. He shoveled their poop. The bunnies huddled together in a corner, like they were afraid of him when he entered with his bucket and shovel. They looked away. That made Ant sad.

Sometimes they would kill one of the bunnies for food. It was the way of things. The nearest stores (and none were very near) had long been emptied; their shelves were bare save for dead insects. The only thing to be found in towns now was death, traveling on two legs, four legs, sometimes more. If you were lucky, death might be fast but luck was an ice-veined bitch that had gone on vacation without leaving a forwarding address. Humanity had gone underground and had yet to dig itself out.

It was best to grow your own if you wanted to survive. But man did not live by root vegetables, berries and tree bark soup alone. The bunnies were a commodity, one you fought to have and struggled to keep. They were a commodity best kept secret.

Ant hated the killing more than anything. Pops made him help, figured it was a reality check. You needed some blood beneath the nails. Made the food taste better, according to Pops. Pops called it "supper time." More like "suffer time." Ant would hold the bunny, forcing its head down, and his father would hit the poor bunny with a claw hammer until it was dead. It always took more than one swing. Ant remembered the first time he swung the hammer, his father yelling at him.

"Swing that motherfucker, Goddamn it! Swing as hard as you can! No reason to make it any worse than it is. Hard and fast! It's just an animal! Christ, it's just an animal."

Ant couldn't do it. He thought he was going to be sick. His hand shook so bad he couldn't even hold the hammer, let alone muster the strength to swing. It kept falling from his grasp. Exasperated and hoarse, Pops gripped his hand in his own and forced the swing.

Pops grunted, "It's yours to finish."

Tears streaking his face, Ant swung as hard as he could. The hammer found its target. It was the worst sound ever. The bunny shuddered. Ant gently stroked the bunny, hoping to calm its death throes. His palm came away red. After some time, he proceeded to skin it.

Due to the lodge's location, they rarely had visitors, fortunately for the visitors. Visitors were more likely to be greeted with a bullet to the head than a hello and there was a special wing for visitors that could attest to that. Eight bodies were buried in unmarked graves. Ant was a good shot. He could thank the hours of forced target practice with the Old Man for that.

The last visitor fortunate enough to avoid a trip to the visitors' wing was a gentleman who looked like Liberace's scarecrow, long dirty-blonde hair, dirty shirt and dirtier jeans and a sequined jacket to shame a Las Vegas showgirl. He just appeared one day, a silhouette in their doorframe, long and lean, like a cobra just before the strike. The cobra knocked on the door, said, "You got a hole in your fence. Couple miles that way. Made for one hell of a short cut but you strike me as a dude who might trip at the thought of trespassers or Jehovah Witnesses. And me, I ain't witnessed Jehovah since I saw these twin brunette sisters in the back room of a club in Toledo and the things they could do… Let's just say if the Olympics gave medals for kink… solid gold, baby. Solid gold."

And so they were introduced to Toxic Tom.

He claimed to be just a traveling minstrel and had a guitar to prove it. He rode a one-horned, one-eyed ex-rodeo bull he called Buttermilk that was bigger and blacker than a stack of Marshall amps, arrived with a thunderstorm at his back and carried silver revolvers he said were haunted.

"They will turn any living thing into a ghost and never apologize," he said with a wink of a bloodshot eye.

He introduced the guns as Chuck and Clint and said they had saved his ass more times than he'd OD'ed.

Tom was a talker. He told road stories back when roads were still usable, going from town to town "using, boozing and cruising the self-destruction highway" before everything went to all white noise, feedback and batfuck.

"This old rock star went nova long before the rest of the world burnt out," the Toxic one said.

"I lived in a black hole for a long time and when the rest of the world finally caught up to me, it was a wake up call, like my muse—dirty, crazy, sexy bitch she is—suddenly realized it was Saturday night and Mama was in the mood to party. I started the tour up again, minus the band, and it's been nonstop ever since. 'Course, the crowds are a smidgen smaller now."

Tom had a tattoo of Jesus on his shoulder but the savior was dressed in black and gold spandex and was minus the beard. When Ant questioned him about the tattoo, Tom said, "Boy, that's ain't Jesus. That's Diamond David Lee Roth, the greatest frontman to ever man a mic, present company excluded, and that, my friend, is the gospel."

Ant and Pops were wary of the wild man but to be honest, it had been months since they had talked to anyone other than themselves. He was a much-needed distraction, one they hoped wouldn't prove dangerous.

"Cute little things, aren't they?" he remarked when he first saw the bunnies. "Always wondered why they said rabbit feet were lucky. Sure as hell wasn't lucky for the rabbit."

They kept him away from the bunnies as much as possible.

Ant was fascinated by Tom. He was as attentive as a dog waiting for scraps when Tom told his stories. He showed them his trinkets from his travels: a big horse-shoe-shaped magnet he claimed to be a "pussy magnet;" bobble heads of Cher, Satan, Frankenstein's Monster, Black Jesus and Superman (one couldn't have enough saviors, Tom claimed); and a six-pack of WWII incendiary grenades acquired from a former Klansman. He no longer had need of them anymore (the apocalypse had come and gone and all colors got corn-holed, according to his Whiteness).

Toxic Tom traveled where the muse and music directed him. Both had been strangely quiet as of late. But it was turning colder, so Tom and Buttermilk had headed south.

"This Freebird needs a tan, not frostbite. Can't solo with frozen fingers."

Most cities had regressed to one step shy of caveman. The law was shoot first, then shoot again if needed. More than anything else, people were scared, looking for anything to latch on to, any glimmer of hope. Problem was most of the anchors available would only drown your sorry ass. Hope was out there but you had a better chance of finding a virgin after a Toxic Tom concert.

Tom's recent journey had crossed paths with the Disciples of the Black Feather. Tom said the Disciples of the Black Feather were a carrion cult that worshipped some god they called Neophron.

Strange religions had evolved from the ashes of the old order, some due to necessity, others just to justify parishioners' actions. Murder was a little easier when it's to appease the appetites of a deity. The carrion cult was one of the more despicable. They were the first to turn to the cemeteries and funeral homes for snacks.

After a time, even the dead weren't given the respect of a proper burial. Cremation became the common means of saying farewell. All you needed was gasoline and a match and maybe a prayer. Even then you had to worry the send off might be crashed by ghouls looking for a barbeque.

Tom said they were nice enough dudes at first until they started salivating, then it was time to go.

"Jerky-eyed motherfuckers tried to put the bite on me. Toxic Tom don't swing that way. No way, honcho. I gave them something to chew on. It was a shoot out at the Far-from-OK Corral. Me and Chuck and Clint went shooting for assholes, and assholes always make good targets."

Tom stayed a few days before moving on. "I can't keep my fans waiting," he grinned as he mounted Buttercup and departed for the next tour stop wherever the hell that was.

" 'Sides, I think I finally figured out how the pussy magnet works, and I hate to delay a lady from paradise. Happy Trails."

And with that he and Buttermilk were "vamonos."

Tom turned out to be a rock star-turned-Nostradamus. Not long after his departure, more strangers came. All three dressed in long, black coats like the shadow man had worn. The shadow man was a figure barely remembered from Ant's childhood dreams.

The shadow man talked about wrath and sin and God and salvation, words Ant didn't understand then and didn't fully understand now. He had given Ant a stick of bubble gum before the Old Man told him to "Get the fuck on your way" and hadn't been seen again.

He sometimes wondered if the shadow man had taken up residence in the visitors' wing.

Sometimes Ant wondered if he had just imagined the whole thing.

The strangers introduced themselves via megaphone, said they were hoping to parley. Ant wasn't sure what that meant. They said they had food and water and were willing to trade. Pops tried to ignore them but it was like trying to ignore cancer; no good was going come of it either way.

Pops agreed to meet but made them strip naked first. They grudgingly complied; one of the strangers kept palming his balls like he was NBA bound. Pops kept his gun in plain view; he wasn't fucking around. Ant stayed behind but well within shooting distance.

True to their word, the strangers did have food. They threw peace offerings: cans of green beans, creamed corn, hash and tomato sauce. The strangers had heard about the bunnies. (Truth be told, a survivor from the shoot out had been tracking Tom, hoping for revenge.) They wanted the bunnies, desired them. They were willing to trade food, clothing, gas, you name it. Hell, they were willing to pay "cold-hearted cash" for the bunnies. Pops didn't want the "cold-hearted cash;" he wanted to keep the bunnies. What the fuck could "cold-hearted cash" buy? Ant didn't know. Ant didn't want the men to have the bunnies either. The look in their eyes reminded him too much of the Old Man after he'd been drinking. The men wouldn't listen. They said they'd "fuggin' take 'em" and began to scale the fence.

The fat one, who had done most of the talking and looked like a bloated, bald possum, was about to say something else when the back of his head exploded. Ant was deadly accurate with the gun.

The other two attempted a hasty retreat. Ant managed to drop one, lead-induced heart attack, and Pops shot Nutgrabber in the crotch. Then to silence his screaming, another for his head.

It was all a distraction.

Ant was closer. He heard the bunnies screaming. He ran, not bothering to wait for Pops and was witness to nightmare.

Three more strangers were at the cage stealing the bunnies. They wore feathers; some stitched through their skin or roach-clipped to their ears. The source of the feathers had accompanied them. It was the scariest thing Ant had ever seen. Its pink head was featherless, heavily scarred, one eye gone. Heavy chain circled its neck. Its talons were as long as the shotgun. The wings once majestic now worn and weary, flapped in excitement. The beak was the color of rust and buried inside one of the bunnies. For Neophron the flightless god, life was measured one meal to the next. And it planned to feast.

Ant took aim when a fourth Black Feather ghoul kicked his legs out from under him. The goon had feathers in place of eyebrows, some kind of avian fashion faux pas. Ant would have laughed had he not been so focused on not having his brains stomped out. Ant crab-walked in reverse, barely avoiding a boot to the face. He got to his feet and ran to where he kept his cleaning supplies

Ant's shovel served a different purpose, almost severing Featherface's head from body with one mighty World Series swing. Blood sprayed and splattered. The bunnies screamed. Featherface dropped like a limp dick in front of barbed wire cunts.

Pop's had finally caught up. He fired first at the carrion god and then at its followers, killing one instantly.

He swung and stuck a hammer, claw end first, inches deep in the nearest stranger's throat, Beardo, christened in lieu of a birth certificate, suffered the steel serpent strike, his beard stained a deep red. Beardo danced like a barnyard chicken. Pops swung the hammer into Beardo's throat once more, jerking towards Hell with each thrust.

The final stranger was well armed; two heavily muscled arms gripped Pops by the throat while the remaining freak arm, retrieved the hammer from Beardo. Hammer removed, Beardo's trachea millimetered towards collapse, Freaker hugged the breath from Pops body. Ant watched his father's body limp to the ground like a deflated birthday balloon. Pops looked content, like he had just squeezed off a well-deserved fart.

Freaker said, "Jack be nimble, Jack be quick, what's it gonna be, tardo? Suck my dick or Seig Heil to the hammer? Either way, I'm taking the bunnies, you stupid shit."

"What Neophron wants, Neophron gets," bellowed Freaker, tossing the hammer from hand to hand to hand.

Ant didn't understand half of what Freaker said. His only directive, a Heavy Metal psalm, a guitar riff from an absent God, was "Protect the bunnies. Protect the bunnies, no matter the cost."

Freaker lunged hammer first. Forearm met shovel with bone-cracking results. Freaker, one arm fragmented, bone shards on display, was sparse on insults, all breath saved for howls of agony. Ant grabbed his head, like Goliath palming a basketball. Squeezing, breathe in, breathe out, repeat. Freaker's eyes exploded like grapes, multicolored streamers of meat and squishy pulp. Fleshy Forth of July gone awry.

Ant dropped to his knees and bellowed his pain, his loss. The bunnies cowered, huddled together as the vulture continued to gulp hunks of bunny flesh down its gullet, blocking any exit with its girth.

Trapped.

"Ant," a voice whispered.

"Ant." It was Pops still breathing, but just barely.

"You have… to get… to the… house. Others will… be coming."

Ant choked back his tears.

"Use me, boy. It's the only… way."

Pops closed his eyes.

Ant shouldered his father on his back and cautiously approached the bird then sprinted, using his father's corpse as a shield. The beak snapped shut on Pops' head. Using all his strength, Ant managed to squeeze past the ravenous creature and booked it for the house.

Not wasting a second, inside he found what he needed.

Just as the world had changed so had science. Unreachable dreams had become man-made nightmares. Evolution had turned evil. Nature had adapted and attacked but had also nurtured defense mechanisms. Thus was born the porcupine suit. Pops had found their remains, the hide too tough for most scavengers. Foot long spines protruded from the suit, a natural defense easily turned into prickly and deadly offense if needed.

It was definitely needed.

Ant confronted the grounded god, yanking on the remains of its tail feathers. The bird pivoted, striking first to its regret.

It squawked in rage and pain. A mouthful of porcupine.

Neophron recoiled and vomited stomach acid, a corrosive concoction of Botulinum toxin, hog cholera and anthrax bacteria. The suit began to dissolve where the foul puke had landed.

Time for plan B. Pops wasn't much of a drinker but the Old Man had been. Ant threw the first bottle of the Old Man's booze, smashing it against the bird's empty eye socket and another and another.

Enraged the bird rose to its full height, shaking the cage's roof from its foundation causing it to collapse, trapping the god momentarily.

A moment was all Ant needed. Wary of its blistering bile, Ant tossed his sole souvenir from Toxic Tom, one of incendiary grenades down its gullet. He remembered Tom's words when he asked if he could have one.

"You'll blow your fucking head off."

He prayed the damn thing worked, otherwise, as a last resort—skunk bombs.

It did.

Kentucky-fried vulture.

Wiping the gore and feathers from his eyes, Ant wearily walked to where his father's headless carcass rested on the ground, his eyes wide, staring but infinitely empty. Time took notice, held its own watch to petite ear to ensure proper ticking. One moment stretched toward forever and beyond. Ant beckoned the surviving bunnies forward. Eye shut tight but not tight enough to contain escaping tears, Ant inaudibly mouthed the word, "Go." The bunnies remained stationary.

Louder this time, "Go."

No request, an order.

The bunnies slowly move towards the exit, still cautious of the great smoldering bird. One bunny, with blonde fur and pail pink eyes stopped, gripped Ant's hand, all a quiver. Ant could not meet the bunny's eyes but could hear the bunny's words.

"Thank you," and with a twitch of its pinkish nose, the bunny hopped away with the rest of the colony. Ant watched bunny tails bounce in the increasing distance.

ACKNOWLEDGMENTS

Thanks to the publisher for taking a chance,
Prof. Morte for taking the time, and for those, before
and after, who cast the long shadows.

Various stories have been previously published in:

Something Funny Is Going On *Teddy Bear Cannibal Massacre*, Dybbuk Press 2005
Water's Edge *Champagne Shivers*, Sam's Dot Publishing 2010
GodTV *Demonology: Grammaticus Demonium*, Double Dragon Publishing 2004
Rot & Roll *Dark Jesters*, Novello Publishers 2006
The Guests *From the Mouth*, Sonar 4 Publications 2009
Picnic in the Woods The Monsters Next Door 2009
The Fisherman *Vile Things*, Comet Press 2009
Starting Over *Project M.* 2004
The Psychic *Champagne Shivers*, Sam's Dot Publishing 2010
Selling Sea Shells *Strange Stories of Sand and Sea*, Fine Tooth Press 2008
The Better Mousetrap *Twisted Cat Tails*, Coscom Entertainment 2006
My Goth Prom Date *Tooth Decay*, Sonar 4 Publications 2009
Devil's Advocate *Demonology: Grammaticus Demonium*, Double Dragon Publishing 2004
Shop Till You Drop *Dead Men (and Women) Walking*, Bards and Sages Publishing 2006
The Audition *Side Show II*, Sam's Dot Publishing 2010

The author about to undergo
Prof. Morte's cure for writer's block.

Brian Rosenberger's writing has appeared in several anthologies. His poetry has been collected in the chapbook *Poems That Go SPLAT* and more recently in *And For My Next Trick*. He lives in a cellar in Marietta, GA, and writes by the light of captured fireflies.